EXPECTING THE PLAYBOY'S HEIR

Penny Jordan

MILLS
BOON

First published in Great Britain 2005
by Mills & Boon, an imprint of Harlequin (UK) Limited,
Large Print edition 2011
Eton House, 18-24 Paradise Road,
Richmond, Surrey TW9 1SR

© Penny Jordan 2005

ISBN: 978 0 263 22336 1

Harlequin (UK) policy is to use papers that are natural,
renewable and recyclable products and made from
wood grown in sustainable forests. The logging and
manufacturing process conform to the legal environmental
regulations of the country of origin.

Printed and bound in Great Britain
by CPI Antony Rowe, Chippenham, Wiltshire

CHAPTER ONE

Lips light as the touch of a butterfly's wings, but far more sensual, brushed the back of her neck, a male hand on her shoulder enclosing the small intimacy in protective secrecy, before he whispered in her ear.

'Back in a few minutes. Don't go away.'

She hadn't moved, not even to turn her head to look at him, and she didn't move now. Mainly because she couldn't, Jules realised shakily.

There were times when she would rather be anything other than one of the partners in an event planning organisation. And this was definitely one of them.

Everyone who was anyone in the celebrity world was here in Majorca, thronging the grounds of the exclusive holiday villa currently on loan to the most excitingly 'in' Hollywood superstar couple.

A-List Life, the magazine responsible for paying for this particular 'bash,' which was ostensibly being given to celebrate the couple's first wedding anniversary, had already described them as Hollywood Royalty.

Now their carefully selected celebrity 'friends' were 'celebrating,' whilst the magazine's flamboyant owner and editor, Dorland Chesterfield, interviewed the happy couple and its photographers mingled with the guests.

She was getting too cynical, Julia decided. Lucy, her friend and the owner of Prêt a Party, had been thrilled about this commission, and of course Julia could understand why.

Dorland was a millionaire and was *the* most influential person on the upmarket social event scene. Being hired to organise any event the magazine was sponsoring—never mind being selected, as they had been, to organise Dorland's fabulous and high-profile end-of-summer celeb bash—was virtually a licence to print money, via future commissions, as Nick, Lucy's husband, had said.

A small frown pleated Julia's forehead as she remembered Nick's unkind comments about Dorland.

'The man's a fat, brainless star-sucker—if he is a man,' he had announced derisively when Dorland had first approached them.

'That's neither true nor fair, Nick.' Julia had immediately defended Dorland.

Yes, Dorland was slightly overweight, and it was true that there were rumours that prior to bursting onto the social scene and setting up his magazine he had undergone a sex-change operation, as well as equally unproven gossip and speculation about his sexual orientation. However, Julia privately suspected he might well be one of those people who genuinely were asexual. Although he was surrounded by eager wannabes of both sexes, thanks to the success of *A-List Life*, no one had ever been able to say categorically that he had had any sexual involvements or partnerships. It was Julia's belief that Dorland reserved all his passion for the great love in his life, which was fame and those who achieved it. Whatever his sexuality, Dorland could tap into the female psyche, and he also had the knack of massaging a vulnerable and famous ego to the point where even the most out-of-reach 'star' was prepared to let down their guard with him.

The truth was that Dorland genuinely liked and admired the famous, and they, sensing that, turned to him and his magazine with the kind of exclusive articles that had other editors gnashing their teeth with envy.

Nick affected to loathe and despise him, but Julia couldn't help wondering if secretly Nick was jealous of both his success and his wealth.

She, not Nick, was the one who had had the headache of organising and co-ordinating the two lavish events Dorland had hired them for. Including dealing with more mammoth egos than any sane person would ever want to know. Nick had cleverly managed to be away chasing up new business or interviewing potential new clients when all the really hard work had had to be done. Nick *was* here today, though.

A pang of pain mingled with guilt squeezed her heart.

There had been a time when in her heart, if not in public, she had begun to dream that she and Nick would become a pair. When he had dropped her for Lucy, shortly after she had introduced them, she had naturally done her best to conceal how she felt, assuring herself that hearts did not break, and that if hers was so very badly cracked that she felt it would never mend, then that was her own affair.

Her mental choice of the word *affair* made her grimace. Nick might have pursued and flattered her, but things had not got to the point where they had exchanged anything more than a few passionate kisses, and thankfully she had not had time to confide in her friends about how she'd felt about him.

But just recently Nick had started to complain to her that his marriage was in difficulties and he felt he had made a mistake. Lucy, too, whilst fiercely loyal to her husband and her marriage, had begun to look strained and unhappy.

After a thorough visual scan, to ensure that nothing needed her attention, Julia was just about to go inside and check on the progress of the interview when Nick came up behind her and put his hand on her bare shoulder again, deliberately caressing the smooth, lightly tanned skin.

'Don't, Nick.' She warned him off.

He ignored her, murmuring tauntingly, 'Don't? Don't what? Don't stop? You know you want it every bit as much as I do.'

'That's not true,' she denied fiercely. 'Apart from anything else, you're married to Lucy.'

'Don't remind me.'

Automatically Julia felt herself recoil. These were words she just did not want to hear, just as this was a situation she did not want to be in, but Nick was still holding her, and closing the gap between them as he whispered thickly, 'Remember how good it was between us? What are you holding back for? Why shouldn't we enjoy one another when it's what we both want? I could come to your room later. No one need know, and—'

'No! It's over between us, Nick. I mean that. And I won't change my mind.'

'Oh, yes, you will,' he told her softly. 'You know that, and so do I.'

He was bending his head towards her and in another heartbeat he would be kissing her.

Panic and guilt invaded her. The last time he had kissed her had been under a tropical moon in the garden of the luxury hotel where they had met, and where she had assumed they would become lovers. But by the end of the holiday Lucy had been the one Nick had declared he loved. Lucy had been the one he had married. Lucy was his *wife*. And one of her two closest friends. No way was she going to betray that friendship. Every marriage went through a bad patch.

Somehow she managed to wrench herself away from Nick, but she had barely taken a couple of steps when she felt hard male fingers gripping her arm.

'No, Nick. I meant what I said,' she said sharply, without bothering to turn her head.

'Did you? He certainly didn't seem to think so—and neither do I!'

'Silas!'

Her whole body went into shock as she stared up in consternation at the man holding on to her.

'How—?' she began, only to be cut off with ruthless efficiency.

'How much did I overhear? All of it,' he told her succinctly. 'How long has it been going on?'

'Nothing is going on!'

The look he gave her—ice-blue eyes narrowed, cynicism tightening his mouth, even the angle of his head as he turned it toward her—reflected his disbelief. She could feel the old familiar mix of anger and antipathy taking hold of her.

'It's true,' she insisted. 'I met Nick before he met Lucy, and the relationship he was referring to was that relationship—not that it's any of your business.'

'A relationship he obviously now believes you want to resume,' Silas said silkily.

'Well, he believes wrong. Because I don't.'

The way he was looking at her was driving up her own anger. They'd never got on, not really. She only tolerated him because of Gramps, whose title and land he would one day inherit.

In Gramps's shoes, she doubted that she would have been able to take to her heart so warmly this American outsider who, by virtue of being descended in the male line from Gramps's younger brother, would one day inherit his title and land. But then she did not possess her grandfather's sanguine outlook on life.

'But you do want *him*.'

It was a taunt rather than a question.

'No!' she said furiously. 'Nick is married to Lucy. And she is my best friend.'

'I know that. But I also know that if you want what you're saying you do, you'll make damn sure he knows that you aren't available.'

Julia had had enough. 'By doing what, exactly?' she demanded angrily.

Silas gave the kind of shrug that only very tall, very muscular, very *male* men could give. And, as always, being forced to recognise his maleness triggered a frisson of awareness inside her that hiked up her antipathy towards him. He had no right to be so damn sexy. It was somehow all wrong that a man who aggravated her as much as Silas did should possess the kind of physique and looks that made grown women react like hormone-controlled teenagers.

'By doing whatever it takes. Either by giving up your job—'

'I won't do that,' Julia interrupted him irritably. 'Especially as Lucy's already lost Carly, now that she's married to Ricardo and expecting a baby. I can't leave as well.'

'—or by making sure Blayne knows you aren't available.'

'I've already told him that I'm not.'

'But, as he can quite plainly see, you are. On the other hand, if there were another man in your life...'

'But there isn't.'

'So find one who's willing to pretend to be there for long enough to get Nick Blayne to back off.'

'What? Like who?'

'Like me.'

'*What?*' Julia shook her head in violent denial. 'You? No. No way! Ever. Absolutely not. Anyway, everyone knows that we loathe one another.'

'It isn't unheard of for couples to discover that what they thought was love is really loathing, so why shouldn't we have made the discovery the other way around?'

'I can't believe I'm hearing this. Do you really expect me to agree to pretend that you and I are in a relationship?'

'I thought you said you wanted to protect Lucy's marriage.'

'I do, but not by offering myself up as a sacrifice for you to devour.'

'Very bacchanalian imagery. Although I confess the thought of you offering yourself up...'

'I wouldn't. Not to you. Not ever.'

'But you would to Nick Blayne?'

'No!'

'So prove it.'

Julia glared at him.

'Just what is this all about, Silas? What's in it for you?' she demanded trenchantly. 'And what on earth are you doing here, anyway? You hate this kind of thing.'

'I'm here because you're here.' Another shrug, more lazily dismissive this time, and the movement of powerful shoulders beneath the linen suit jacket unbelievably and very much unwantedly conjured up images of just such a pair of male shoulders naked, and gleaming in the morning sunlight as their owner arched his equally naked and male body over her own.

Silas naked?

Such an image might not be legally or even morally taboo, but it was certainly not the way she was used to thinking about him. Was this the kind of thing that happened when you were in your mid-twenties and your sex life was an arid desert, refreshed only by watching reruns of *Sex and the City* and determinedly refusing to study the ads in the back of glossy magazines for purveyors of sex toys?

'Oh, yes. Of course,' she agreed wryly, hurriedly banishing her unexpectedly erotic mental images.

But before she could ask him why he was really there, he told her coolly, 'You should wear a hat in this heat. Your face is burning.'

Maybe it was, but the heat it was giving off hadn't been caused by the sun, Julia admitted to herself.

That was the trouble with Silas. Much as he filled her with wary dislike and suspicion, she still couldn't stop herself from being aware of him as a man. And not just any man, but a very dangerously sexy man.

'What is it you really want?' she demanded.

'Well, for one thing I want your grandfather's peace of mind and continued good health. We both know how much it would upset him if it got into the papers—as it more than likely would—that his beloved granddaughter was involved in a sordid love triangle. And for another... Let's just say that it would be convenient for me right now to be seen publicly as romantically involved.'

It might not, Silas had decided in his practical way, be in his own best interests to discuss Aimee DeTroite and the problems she was causing him with Julia. There was no need, after all, for her to have to know. And as for Aimee herself—since she continued to take such an unwanted and intrusive interest in his private life, hopefully the discovery that he was now 'coupled up' with Julia should send a very clear message to her that she was wasting her time.

Not that that was the only or even the most important reason he had for what he was doing.

'Well, at least you haven't claimed that you want me,' Julia told him.

'Would you like me to?'

Say it or mean it? Julia felt her heart ricochet from one side of her chest to the other.

'It might be worth it, just for the pleasure of calling your bluff,' she told him sweetly.

'Like Blayne was calling yours, you mean?' Silas challenged her.

'I meant what I said to him,' Julia told him hotly.

'Then prove it.'

'I don't have to prove anything to you.'

'Not to me, perhaps,' he agreed, in that mocking way of his that so infuriated her. 'But I rather think that you do have something to prove to Lucy. She was standing right next to me when Blayne was kissing your neck.'

Immediately, and anxiously, she looked beyond his shoulder to where she could see Lucy, talking to the magazine editor.

'She saw him?' she demanded, concern for her friend immediately pushing everything else she was feeling out of the way.

'Yes.'

Lucy, her lifelong friend. Lucy, who always somehow seemed to be struggling to conceal an inner fragility and vulnerability. Lucy, who would be broken and destroyed by the thought that her husband was cheating on her with her best friend. No way could she allow that to happen, no matter what temporary sacrifices she might have to make herself.

'Very well, then. I'll do it,' she told him impetuously. It would be worth it to protect her friend's marriage. And to assuage her own guilt?

CHAPTER TWO

'AH! HERE you are!'

Julia hoped that her expression hadn't betrayed how very unloverlike and ill at ease Silas's appearance had caused her to feel, coupled with his warm, husky greeting—somehow as sensually intimate as though he had addressed her in far more loverlike terms—and the weight of Silas's arm around her shoulders.

'Missed me?'

Two words and one look, focused on her eyes and then dropping to her mouth, one small touch of male fingers in her hair. Dammit, Silas should have been an actor. He was certainly putting on an Oscar-worthy performance. Even her own body had been taken in by it.

And as for either Lucy or Dorland Chesterfield guessing they were putting on an act—if their expressions of delighted astonishment were anything to go by they were far too excited to notice anything other than what Silas wanted them to see.

'Jules!' Lucy squeaked. 'Why on earth didn't you tell me?'

Dorland mopped his round sweating face with his handkerchief, and then breathed happily, 'Oh, my, what a potentially delectable feast of delicious gossip. Billions of dollars, a title, and the fact that the two of you are related. Perfect.'

'Dorland...' Julia began apprehensively, but her caution was lost in Silas's words.

'We haven't known for very long ourselves, have we?'

Automatically she turned towards him. He must have been right about the heat, because suddenly she felt distinctly odd, sort of dizzy and light-headed, whilst her heart fluttered in shallow little beats. How was he managing to look every bit as arrogant and potently male as he always did? He was focusing on her with a gaze of such sensual hunger that it actually made the colour rise up under her skin.

'Jules, you're blushing!' Lucy exclaimed, laughing.

This was ridiculous!

'We said that we were not going to go public yet—remember,' she told Silas, forcing herself to soften her voice to an unfelt sweetness whilst returning his look with one of her own that was not so much ardent as reproachful.

'I wasn't aware that we had,' Silas countered, causing Lucy to laugh.

'Just the way you're looking at Jules says it all, Silas. If ever a man's gaze said *I love you and I want you in bed*, yours just did.'

'Mmm… Well, it has been a while,' Silas answered shamelessly, and Julia longed for the privacy to tell him exactly what she thought of his enthusiasm for his new role.

'You'll have to take some time off from that Foundation of yours and spend it with Julia instead,' Dorland chipped in.

Julia looked at him in triumph and waited. No way would Silas do that. He was caught neatly in his own lies, and it served him right.

His hand had moved from her shoulder to her neck, and his fingers were stroking into her hair. She had to fight against an instinctive desire to stretch luxuriously into his touch, demanding more of it.

'That's exactly what I intend to do. In fact, that's exactly what I am doing. From now on where Jules goes, I go.'

'You can't do that,' Julia objected, panicking. 'I'm working.'

The hard fingers weren't stroking now, but pressing warningly instead.

'Of course, but not twenty-four hours a day. And when you aren't working...'

'Silas, don't you dare take her away from me until the end of the year,' Lucy begged. 'We've got so much work on I couldn't manage without her—especially now that Dorland has asked us to organise his big summer party.'

'You've got her until the end of the year,' Silas agreed. 'But, as I've just said, where Jules goes, I go—and her off-duty time is mine.'

Lucy burst out laughing. 'Silas, you *must* be in love. I thought you hated parties and huge events.'

'I do, but I love Julia more than I loathe them.'

She had had enough, Julia decided—more than enough, and in spades.

'Darling, I can't possibly let you make such a sacrifice. Of course you mustn't do any such thing. You'd be bored to tears, hanging around waiting for me. And besides, we are going to spend the rest of our lives together.' She smiled sweetly and waited. She could see the 'I take no prisoners' glint in Silas's eyes, but no way was she going to back down.

'How could being with you ever be a sacrifice?' His arm was round her waist and he had closed the distance between them, holding her against him, his free hand resting on her hip, which he was rubbing tenderly in a gesture of supposedly subtle intimacy.

'No, my mind is made up. Unless Lucy objects, where you go, I go.'

'Of course I don't object,' Lucy assured him.

'You've got the Silverwoods' combined silver wedding and eighteenth for their son coming up next, haven't you, Jules? That is going to be huge, I know.' She hesitated, and then said diffidently, 'Nick mentioned to me that you'd hinted that you'd like him to give you some support with it, and—'

'No! I mean, there's no need for him to do that.' She could hardly tell Lucy that she had said no such thing, and that Nick had lied to her. 'Nick must have misunderstood what I was saying.'

Lucy might be looking relieved and smiling, but Julia noticed that Silas certainly wasn't mirroring Lucy's response.

'And don't forget my end-of-summer bash,' Dorland broke in.

'Yes, you're doing that, Jules,' Lucy agreed. 'And I'll do all the smaller UK-based stuff— which will leave you with just the Sheikh's post-Ramadan party in Dubai.'

'Fine.' Did her voice and face sound and look as tight as they felt? 'But right now it's time for the buffet to be served, plus I've got to organise champagne for the toast and check that everything's set for the firework display. So if you'll all excuse me...'

She turned to walk away and then found that she couldn't. Silas had somehow taken her hand in his and entwined his fingers through her own in a pseudo-lover's clasp that effectively locked her to him like a prisoner.

Indignation flashed hotly in the irate glare Jules gave him, turning the normal amber of her eyes to a brilliant speckled gold.

But Silas ignored her outrage, just as he ignored the rejecting shake of her head and the resultant shiny disorder of her blonde hair, with its streaks of dark gold.

'Silas,' she began, through gritted teeth, but stopped as he raised their clasped hands to his lips and then opened her palm and pressed a very deliberate and very sensual kiss into it.

Shock, heat, and a surge of lust she would never in a thousand lifetimes have associated with her true feelings towards Silas rampaged through her, leaving her in possession of the unwanted discovery that knees *did* go weak and that desire *was* a shockingly unfathomable and treacherous thing.

When Silas released her, her body felt as giddy and unstable as though she had consumed a whole bottle of Cristal champagne. She made a valiant effort not to simply stand and stare at him.

Dorland's photographers were still swarming all over the place, chasing down celebrities for the photographs that the magazine's readers pored over so eagerly, and so too were the legions of PRs, make-up artists, hairdressers, personal trainers, dressers, astrologers... No right-thinking superstar would dream of being without his or her entourage.

The white powder so beloved amongst the foibles of the foolish and famous had also been very much in evidence during the big event, and Julia had lost count of the number of times she had refused offers of 'something'.

To those who loved reading celebrity magazines the lifestyle of those they read about might seem enviable and glamorous, but the reality was that beneath the glitter and excitement lay a deep and dark abyss into which today's star could all too easily disappear and be forgotten.

'Thank God Tiffany relented and allowed Martina to borrow that diamond necklace she'd set her heart on wearing,' she heard Dorland remark.

'Only thanks to you,' Julia pointed out, determinedly not looking at Silas.

'Well, like I told them, they'd be missing a terrific PR opportunity if they refused,' Dorland agreed happily.

'Perhaps they were more concerned about the possibility of missing a few million dollars' worthy of diamond necklace,' Silas pointed out dryly. 'After all, it would not be the first time a star has ''lost'' a valuable piece of jewellery she's only had on loan.'

'Oooh, Silas, that is so naughty of you.' Dorland pouted theatrically. 'What kind of ring are you going to give our Julia? Something new and shiny? Or is it going to be a family heirloom? I heard on the grapevine that you've hunted down most of the stuff your mutual great-great-grandfather gambled away—and paid enough to cover the national debt of a small country for it,' he added gleefully.

'Silas, you haven't?' Julia protested.

'The sapphire and diamond set presented to our great-great-grandmother on her betrothal is of considerable historical value, and as such reassembling it was a worthwhile project.'

Julia's eyes widened. '*All* of it?'

A certain Indian Maharajah had presented the jewellery to the bride, with whom, as rumour had it, he had fallen passionately in love. The household records her grandfather had shown her when he had told her the story had listed the gift as comprising not just the expected necklace, earrings, bracelets and tiara, but in addition matching jewelled combs and brushes, along with perfume bottles and a gem-studded carrying case. The necklace itself had contained seven sapphires unique in colour and size.

'All of it,' Silas agreed.

'Ah, Julia, my dear, you are so fortunate. Your very own billionaire. What fun!'

Fun? Silas? Julia didn't think so. No way could she ever envisage using such a lightweight word as *fun* in connection with a man who was predominantly and dangerously a heavyweight alpha male.

What would he be like in bed?

Her curiosity caught her unprepared with its small provocative question.

'I must go. I've got a meeting with the PR people,' she fibbed, cravenly making her escape.

Inside the villa, the 'happy couple' were still being interviewed, looking anything but happy.

Love! The older she got, the less she believed it actually existed, Jules reflected cynically as she went to warn the caterers that it was time to start serving the buffet.

The villa hired for the anniversary party had originally belonged to an eccentric art collector who had had it built early in the twentieth century to house his collection of Greek and Roman artefacts. It was built on a small promontory overlooking the sea, in a design vaguely reminiscent of a Roman villa, around an enclosed courtyard complete with marble columns and a sunken pool.

The plan was that as the sun set the celebrating celebrities would reaffirm their vows on the sea-facing terrace outside the villa, the light of the sun to be replaced by the light of the one thousand and one candles inside the villa and the inner courtyard.

They had had terrific problems getting the people who owned the villa to agree to the lit candles, and Julia was hoping that she had organised enough candle-lighters to get them all lit at the same time. The idea was that the first one in every ten would be lit first, then the second, and so on until they were all burning.

She just hoped it was going to work.

Her palm was still tingling where Silas had kissed it. *Kissed* it. He had done much more than that, she reminded herself indignantly, as she remembered the way his tongue-tip had stroked a fiery circle of erotic pleasure over her skin.

His expertise had suggested that he would be a very accomplished lover. But would he be sensual and passionate? Would he give himself to the need he aroused in his partner? Would he…?

Not that she was interested in knowing, of course. No way would she ever flutter her eyelashes and fawn over a man the way she had seen the girls he had brought down to Amberley do.

She had still been a schoolgirl then, resenting the fact that Silas's annual summer visit to Amberley coincided with her own time there. And aware too that whilst for now Amberley was *her* home, one day it would belong to Silas.

Now it was not the potential loss of Amberley that hurt, but rather the potential loss of her grandfather. Her mother was the child of his second marriage, and he was in his seventies now, his heart weakened by the serious heart attack he had suffered eighteen months ago.

He was so precious to her, and so loved. He had provided her with the male influence in her life after her parents' divorce, and at the same time he had given her and her mother a home.

Her mother had remarried three years ago, and, though Jules liked her stepfather, he could never take the place of her grandfather.

What exactly had Silas meant when he had said that it would suit him to be in a relationship? One day he would have to marry, if he wanted to provide an heir for Amberley—and Jules felt sure that he would want to do so. He was in his thirties now, and he was not the kind of man who would flinch from telling a woman that his relationship with her was over.

Like her, Silas had grown up without his father. Not because his parents had been divorced, as her own had been, but because his father had been killed in a freak sailing accident when Silas had only been a few months old.

She looked down at the floor, not wanting to think of Silas as a vulnerable fatherless baby, and then frowned as she studied her shoes. Shopping was her Achilles' heel and shoes were her downfall, and had been all her life. She still had, in their original shoe boxes, the pretty dancing shoes she had persuaded her mother to buy for her as a child, and tomorrow morning she was hoping to be able to slip away to visit a local shop, where she had heard it was possible to pick up exclusive samples of shoes from one of fashion's hottest new young designers.

The sun was beginning to set. The celebrity couple emerged on to the steps of the impressive portico to the villa, she with her head thrown back and her throat arched, to reveal the glitter of the Tiffany necklace as she leaned into her husband, and he gazing adoringly down at her. They were presenting a very different image from the one Jules had seen earlier in the day, when she had been screaming at him, accusing him of cheating on her, whilst he had snarled back that she was so self-obsessed he was surprised she had even noticed.

'It would have been hard not to, darling. Not when the little slut in question was supposed to be my manicurist. Except it wasn't a *nail* job she was giving you when I walked into the bedroom and found you with her, was it?'

Now the slender, supple female figure—kept that way, so rumour had it, by a rigorous regime of drugs reinforced by cosmetic surgery—was angled towards her husband's, whilst his hand rested possessively on her hip.

Jules heard Lucy, who was standing next to her, give a small sad sigh. Poor Lucy, married to a man who had no respect either for her or the vows he had made to her. And where was Nick anyway?

Automatically Julia turned her head to look for him, almost jumping out of her skin when she heard Silas demanding, 'Looking for someone?'

'Yes—you, of course, darling,' she responded with sugary sweetness.

'Girls, this is great,' Dorland enthused as he lumbered towards them, mopping the perspiration from his face with a large handkerchief.

The sun was setting, the photographers were busily snapping away as the celebs reaffirmed their vows, and in their tens, twenties and hundreds the lights of the candles glowed against the warm Mediterranean darkness.

Silas looked on, and murmured, 'What a total farce.'

'It's supposed to be very romantic and symbolic,' Julia pointed out crossly.

'I'm astonished that you managed to get insurance for something like this.' Silas grimaced.

'Nick dealt with the insurance,' Julia told him absently, before demanding, 'You didn't really mean what you said to Dorland and Lucy, did you?'

'Which bit?'

All of it, Julia was tempted to say, but instead she answered, 'The bit that went ''Where Jules goes, I go''. I mean, it's bad enough that you said anything to Dorland at all—'

'Why?'

'*Why?*' She stared at him in disbelief. 'Silas, Dorland owns *A-List Life*. He gets off on going public on personal stuff that people want to keep private.'

'Like Nick Blayne and you, you mean?'

Julia hissed in angry disbelief. 'There is no Nick Blayne and me.'

'Blayne doesn't seem to think that. Which would you rather have, Julia? Dorland publishing a coy announcement that you and I are an item, or Dorland hinting that you and Blayne are having an affair behind his wife's back?'

'Neither,' Julia told him shortly. 'Silas, you're going to have to say something to

Dorland and…and tell him that you don't want anyone else to know about us yet.'

'With the ego-driven photo fodder Dorland's assembled here, the last thing he's going to be interested in is us,' Silas told her derisively.

'Shush!' Julia hushed him warningly, looking round quickly to check that no one was standing close enough to him to have overheard him. 'Lucy's business is dependent on people like these, and, since I work for her, so is my job.'

She caught his derisive look and felt compelled to demand, 'What's your real motive for this, Silas? I refuse to believe that you really intend to spend virtually the whole of the next six months policing me just because you don't want to see Lucy hurt or because you disapprove of extra-marital affairs.'

'So you *have* been having an affair with Blayne, then?'

Julia exhaled noisily and fixed him with a furious amber glare.

'Oh, that's just so typical of you—trying to play catch-out by deliberately twisting what

I'm saying to suit your own purposes. No, I'm not having an affair with Nick.'

'Okay, maybe describing it as an affair *is* going too far. You've had sex with him and you want to have sex with him again—is that better?'

'No, it is not. Just in case you've forgotten, Silas, I'm twenty-six—not sixteen.'

'Meaning?'

'Meaning that I'm plenty old enough to have lost my illusions about what sex is really like. A sixteen-year-old might—just might— be starry-eyed and hormone-driven enough to believe that wonderful, mind-blowing, trans- ports-you-to-another-dimension sex actually exists, and to lust after it and the partner she thinks will supply it for her, but a twenty-six- year-old woman knows the truth.'

'Which is?'

Julia gave a small dismissive shrug.

'That the kind of sex we fantasise about as teenagers is just that—a fantasy. Sexual satis- faction isn't a life-changing experience that transports you to some kind of unique physical heaven, and it certainly isn't worth betraying a friendship like mine and Lucy's for. But of course no one wants to admit it. I'm not saying that sex isn't enjoyable. I'm just saying that after the fantasy sex girls build up inside their heads, the reality can be a bit of a let-down.'

'It's an interesting theory, but not one, I suspect, that is shared by the majority of your peers.'

'You'd be surprised,' Julia told him darkly. 'More and more women in their thirties who are in relationships are saying that sex just doesn't interest them any more.'

'Mmm, well, to judge by the antics being indulged in by the majority of the guests here this evening, they are not in agreement with you.'

'Most of them are out of their heads on drink or drugs—or both.'

'Habits you don't share?'

'I've seen too much of what they can do. I like a glass of wine with a meal and the occasional glass of champagne, but that's all. Besides, I couldn't do my job if I was out of my head on drink and drugs.'

The first of the fireworks exploded above their heads in a shimmer of brilliant falling stars, quickly followed by several others.

'I understand from Dorland that you'll be leaving for Italy tomorrow?'

'Yes, I'm flying to Naples and going from there to Positano for my next job. Silas, there's no need for you to come with me. Lucy is bound to tell Nick about us, and seeing us together has certainly reassured her. I hate to think of her being hurt.'

'But ultimately I suspect that she will be, unfortunately,' Silas warned her. 'Her marriage to Blayne makes that inevitable.'

Another firework went off in an explosive crackle of noise that caught Julia off guard, and instinctively she took a step closer to Silas. Immediately he put his arm around her, causing her to turn her head to look up at him.

Silas was looking back at her, his head bent towards her own. A frisson of something unfamiliar and yet oddly instantly recognised by her senses gripped her emotions, causing her eyes to widen. She could feel the warmth of Silas's arm round her and smell the scent of his skin, warm, male, and luring her to move closer to him to breathe it into herself more deeply. A small, sharp spasm of physical shock shook through her. She could feel the rocky, unsteady thud of her own heartbeat. Why had she never noticed before how sexy Silas's mouth was? His lower lip was sensually full, whilst his top lip was so cleanly cut that she had to subdue a crazy impulse to reach out and trace it with her fingertip.

'Blayne's watching us.'

'What?'

It took several seconds for Silas's comment to penetrate the disconcerting confusion of her wandering thoughts, and then several more for her to translate it into an explanation of why Silas was continuing to hold her.

And a reason for the downward movement of his head now, at the same time as he drew her against his body and held her there, one hand in the hollow of her back, pressing her into him, the other splayed against the back of her head, supporting it as the lips she had been admiring brushed coolly against her own.

The temptation was too much for her to resist. Silas's mouth was now hers to explore more intimately. Slowly and carefully she traced their outline with the tip of her tongue. His lips felt cool, and smooth, and firm. A cascade of small quivering shots of delight tumbled down her spine, coupled with a desire for something more. Automatically she moved even closer, and then made a small sound of complaint when Silas stepped back from her.

'If you were doing that for Blayne's benefit,' he began in an almost harsh voice, 'then—'

'Nick's benefit?' Julia realised that she had completely forgotten about Lucy's husband. No way did she want Silas to know that, though.

'I don't know why you sound so disapproving,' she told him airily. 'This whole thing was your idea, after all—although why you should want to protect Lucy...' A sudden thought struck her. 'You aren't doing this for Lucy's sake at all, are you? So why...? Oh, I get it. You're using me to— What's she like, Silas, and why are you going to such lengths to get rid of her?'

'What?' He was frowning impatiently now.

'You heard me,' Julia persisted. 'What's she like, this woman you want to shake off by pretending to be involved with me?'

'What makes you think there is any such woman?'

'What other reason could there be?' Julia answered him practically. 'Although I must admit you've never struck me as the kind of man who'd have any trouble leaving behind anything or anyone he didn't want any more.'

'Thanks.'

'Even Gramps admits that you can be single-minded,' Julia pointed out. 'And he dotes on you. Mind you, I would have thought that you'd be looking for commitment instead of trying to avoid it—or wasn't she the right type to become a countess and the mother of the next Amberley heir?'

'You're jealousy's showing,' Silas warned her.

'What?' Julia gave him an indignant look. 'No way am I jealous of your women.'

Through the darkness Julia could almost feel his quick, almost bruisingly hard visual inspection of her shadowed face in a silence that suddenly seemed to be packed tight with explosive tension.

'I meant your jealousy of the fact that ultimately I will inherit Amberley and not you.'

Julia felt her face start to burn. If she kept on like this Silas would probably start thinking that she was secretly in love with him. And she most certainly was not.

'That's ridiculous,' she defended herself. 'I've always known that you will inherit Amberley.'

'And you've always resented me because of it.'

He made it a fact rather than a question.

'No, I haven't,' Julia objected immediately.

'Liar. Even as a child you went to extraordinary lengths to make it clear to me that I was an outsider.'

Julia frowned. 'That wasn't because you'll inherit Amberley.'

'No?'

'No!' Reluctantly she admitted, 'Ma told me, when I was about six that if Gramps died then she and I would have to find somewhere else to live because Amberley would be yours. I suppose she just wanted to warn me what the situation was, but for a long time I was afraid that I would come back from school one day and Gramps would be dead. Ma always did her best, but sometimes not having a father hurts.'

'Tell me about it.'

Julia glanced at him and then said bleakly, 'Neither of us has had much luck in that department, have we? Your father died when you were only a few months old and landed you with those ancient trustees you inherited from him, and mine took one look at me and left Ma for someone else. Which do you think is worse? Your father being dead or your father being alive but not wanting you?'

To her own irritation, her voice had thickened with the tears blurring her eyes. She had thought she'd talked herself out of this kind of self-pity at junior school.

And even worse than self-pity was the thought of someone else's pity—especially if that someone else was Silas. To forestall any offer of it she pulled away from him, and was startled to discover how much her body resented its removal from the warmth of his.

'I'd better go and check that the candles are all put out properly.' The look he gave her made her point out defensively, 'I am supposed to be working.'

'Working?'

'My job might seem shallow and pointless to you, Silas, and I know that other people envy me because they think I spend all my time mixing with celebrities and partying, but the reality is that neither you nor they appreciate what a tough job this actually is. Lucy's worked very hard to build up this business, and I owe it to her to do my job as professionally as I can.'

'By schmoozing rich old men and their plastic-fantastic Stepford Wife women?' Silas taunted her.

'That's unfair. Corporate and event entertainment is big business—and don't tell me that you haven't hired event organisers yourself, because I won't believe you.'

Some of the billions of dollars Silas's grand-mother's family had earned from oil had been used in his grandfather's time to set up a char-itable arts foundation, which Silas now headed.

Silas gave a small dismissive gesture, his accent suddenly very American as he drawled, 'Sure. We've done stuff—fundraisers at the Met, and in conjunction with the Getty. My mother generally organises them, since she's the head of our fund-raising committee.'

She saw the gleam in his eyes as he looked at her. 'She would have been happy to give you a job—you know that.'

Julia made no comment. Like everyone, apart from Silas himself, Julia was slightly in awe of Silas's charming but formidably orga-nised and successful mother.

'Lucy asked me first, and I couldn't let her down.'

'But you could allow her husband to prop-osition you?'

Julia's mouth compressed.

'Nick and Lucy are going through a bad patch.'

'And having sex with you was going to be a Band-Aid to hold their marriage together?'

Julia didn't bother to make any response, simply walking away from him instead, but his words were very much in her thoughts as she checked that all the candles were being doused properly.

She had felt so envious of Lucy when she and Nick had married, and so determined to make sure that no one guessed how she felt, but just lately she had begun to see Nick in a different light, and to feel sorry for Lucy instead of envying her.

In fact, refusing Nick's blandishments and often openly sexual hints that he wasn't happy in his marriage had proved to be surprisingly easy. Nick made no secret of the fact that he considered himself to be an accomplished lover, openly boasting to her of the pleasure he could give her, but some instinct told her that in bed he would not be in the same class as Silas.

Her face burned hotly with guilt as she recognised the path along which her thoughts were trespassing. Silas's sexual expertise or lack of it was not something she should be thinking about or interested in. After all, he had never shown any kind of sexual interest in her.

Until tonight.

Tonight? That passionless brush of his mouth against her own?

Passionless for him, maybe, but *she* had certainly felt a distinct kick of sexual curiosity galvanising her body.

Don't even think about going there, Julia muttered warningly to herself, and then jumped as Nick materialised at her side and demanded huskily, 'Missed me?'

'Have you been somewhere?' Julia riposted sweetly. 'I've been too busy to notice—although I expect Lucy will be wondering where you are.'

'Well, in the morning you can tell her that I spent the night in your bed, if you want to.'

He was standing in front of her, blocking her in, having placed one hand on the column behind her.

'I've already told you, Nick, I'm not interested.'

'Of course you are. You've been acting like a bitch on heat ever since I dropped you for Lucy.' He was smiling at her as though the words had been a compliment and not an insult, Julia saw, and a surge of angry contempt for him mixed with compassionate pity for Lucy gathered force inside her.

'Really?' She kept her voice deliberately light. 'I must tell Silas that. He'll be delighted to learn that other men are aware of how much I want him.'

Immediately Nick removed his hand from the column behind her.

'Silas?' he demanded. 'You mean Silas is shagging you?'

'We are lovers, yes,' Julia lied firmly. How could she ever have found anything attractive in Nick? Even the way he spoke revealed his contempt for women.

'Why?'

'The usual reasons. He's sexy, and I want him, and—'

'No, I meant why should he want to shag *you*?' Nick told her brutally. 'With his money he could have anyone he wants.'

Her original distaste for Nick's comments was rapidly turning into outright loathing for Nick himself.

'The "anyone" Silas wants is me. And the only man I want is Silas. You, Nick, are married to Lucy. She's my friend, and—'

Julia protested in shock as Nick suddenly grabbed hold of her upper arms and forced her back against the column, shaking her so hard that she only just avoided banging her head on the hard stone.

'Are you sure you don't want it? I think you do. I think you're gagging for it. And I think I should give it to you hot and hard, right here and now. You owe me, Jules, and I intend to collect—one way or another.'

All of a sudden Julia didn't just feel angry and repulsed, but actually afraid. There was an ugly sound to Nick's voice, a miasma of lust and contempt somehow emanating from him. Instinctively she fought to break free of him as he held on to her, twisting and turning, the fragile fabric of her dress tearing beneath his grip. Her furious panic gave her a fierce determination not to give in to him, even though he was hurting her. But it was only when she kicked out at him and her heel caught his leg, that he yelled out in pain and let her go. She could hear him cursing her as he held his calf, and she pushed past him and started to run towards the building and safety, too afraid of him coming after her to turn round to look and see if he was following her.

She was still trembling almost fifteen minutes later in the sanctuary of the ladies' room, where she pulled off her torn dress and re-dressed in the jeans and tee shirt she had been wearing earlier in the day, which she had stuffed, rolled up, into a bag she had left with the caterers.

There would be bruises on her arms in the morning from Nick's assault on her.

Assault. The word tasted gritty and unpleasant in her mouth, but he *had* assaulted her. Would he have raped her if she hadn't broken free and escaped from him? Julia was not a naive teenager. She knew full well that there was a sordid underbelly to the glamourous celebrity lifestyle depicted in magazines such as *A-List Life*, but this was the first time its sleaziness had actively touched her. She had spoken the truth when she had told Silas that she neither drank to excess nor took drugs. In addition, she might not be sexually innocent, but she was very firm about maintaining a professional distancing manner when she was working, and she was most certainly not promiscuous. The drink- and drug-fuelled group sex sessions of the type that featured in the lives of many of their clients, as well as in the more downmarket tabloids, held absolutely no appeal for her.

But she had not been aware of how dangerous Nick was. He was taking her refusal to have sex with him far more personally than she had expected, treating it as though it were a personal strike against him he had to avenge. Shuddering a little as she remembered the horrible way he had spoken to her, and how frightened he had made her feel, Julia bundled her torn dress into the bag that had held her jeans and top. Suddenly Silas's constant presence for the rest of the summer felt more comforting than burdensome. Not, of course, that she would ever tell Silas himself as much.

Along with Lucy and Nick, as well as the catering staff and virtually everyone else who had accompanied them to Majorca, Julia was staying at a small budget-priced hotel in one of the main holiday resorts. She had planned to get a lift back to the hotel with Lucy and Nick but now she knew that nothing would persuade her to do so. Instead she would have to blag a lift with one of the contractors.

'Jules, have you seen Nick anywhere?'

She tensed as she heard the anxiety in Lucy's voice as she came hurrying toward her.

'Not recently,' she answered truthfully.

'He might still be with Alexina Matalos, then,' Lucy sighed. 'She wants us to quote for her husband's fiftieth birthday party. Oh, and Silas was looking for you. I'm so pleased about the two of you.'

'Not as pleased as I am,' said a deep voice.

'Oh, Silas, good. You've found her.' Lucy laughed as he materialised beside them out of the darkness.

'What happened to the dress?' he asked Julia as he smiled in acknowledgment of Lucy's statement.

'I changed it. Jeans are more practical for putting out candles than chiffon.'

'How much longer will it be before you've finished here?'

'I'm virtually done, but there's no need for you to hang around waiting for me, Si... *darling*,' she emphasised, conscious that Lucy was listening to them.

'How are you planning to get back to the hotel?' he asked, ignoring her hint.

'Oh, I'll get a lift with one of the contractors,' Julia told him airily.

'Fine. I'll come with you.'

With her?

She knew they were supposed to be an item, but surely that was taking things too far? Especially when he would then have to make his way back to wherever it was he was staying, which she presumed must be the same ultra-exclusive boutique hotel in Palma as Dorland.

'Well, now that you two have made contact with one another, I'd better go and find Nick,' Lucy announced.

'There's really no need for you to come back to the hotel with me,' Julia repeated as soon as Lucy had gone.

'Julia, we're going now, if you're coming,' one of the contractors called out.

'Can you fit both of us in?' Silas asked him.

'Sure.'

Silas's hand was splayed across the small of her back, urging her forward.

It was funny how, though Silas's hand held far more hard strength than Nick's, she somehow wanted to relax into his touch rather than shrink back from it. That might be funny, but what was definitely not was the discovery that, instead of moving forward, she really wanted to turn sideways instead, and move closer to Silas.

Why? she derided herself, deliberately trying to whip up awareness of her own foolishness. So that she could get another look at his mouth? Another taste of his mouth? But her body's reaction, far from being an appropriate recognition of her folly, was a wilful misunderstanding of the message she was sending it.

It, it seemed, would very much like another taste of Silas.

When had she become the kind of woman who actively liked courting danger?

CHAPTER THREE

'*HOLA*, SEÑOR.' The receptionist beamed up at Silas from behind the desk. 'Here is your key.'

His key? Julia stared at him.

'You aren't staying here?'

Silas was a 'five-star hotel and nothing less' man. No—correction. Silas was a 'private villa and his own personal space' man who, she was pretty sure, had never stayed at a three-star hotel in his life.

'I've booked us a suite and asked them to move your stuff to it from your room. That way Blayne won't be under any misapprehensions about us or our relationship.'

A suite? Us? Their relationship?

'Something wrong?' Silas asked her.

'Do you really need to ask?' Julia challenged him as soon as she had got enough breath back to speak. 'Silas, no way am I going to sleep with you.'

'*Sleep* with me?'

'You know what I mean,' Julia told him crossly.

'We'll discuss it in our suite, shall we?' Silas suggested in a gentle voice that felt like a very thin covering over very hard steel as it fell against her frazzled nerve-endings. 'Unless, of course, you feel that having the hotel staff witness a potential quarrel between us is going to add reality to our relationship?'

Since he was already standing next to her, bending towards her in a way that no doubt looked sensually lover-like to their audience but, Julia nastily decided, was just another example of the dictatorial side of his nature she had always disliked, she didn't have much choice other than to allow him to propel her towards the rackety lift.

'I suppose this wretched suite is on the top floor,' she complained as the lift started to lurch upwards.

'Since Señora Bonita has assured me that it is possible to see the sea from its windows, I imagine that it must be,' Silas concurred, so straight-faced that Julia had to look at him very

carefully to catch the smallest of small betraying quivers lifting the corners of his mouth.

'And you believed her? The sea is miles
away.'

'No doubt the *señora* assumes we will be
far too busy gazing at one another to concern
ourselves over her enthusiastic laundering of
reality.'

'This lift takes for ever, and I'm not even
sure that it's safe,' Julia complained. For some
reason she wasn't prepared to explain, even to
herself, it seemed a very good idea to keep her
gaze concentrated on the lift door and not on
Silas.

'"A long, slow ride to heaven" was how
the *señora* poetically described it to me.'

Forgetting her determination not to look at
him, Julia turned round and accused him,
'You're making that up.'

Silas gave a small shrug.

'Silas, why are you doing this?' Julia demanded, then her eyes widened as the lift suddenly shuddered theatrically and then dropped
slightly, throwing her off balance and against
Silas.

Immediately his arms went round her to steady her, and equally immediately he released her and moved back from her.

'Something wrong?'

Julia glared at him. What was he trying to imply?

'This lift isn't safe,' she told him.

Silas watched the emotions chase one another across her face. She had always had the most expressive eyes, and they were telling him quite plainly now exactly what she thought. Fortunately, he was rather more adept at guarding his own expression, otherwise she would have been able to read equally clearly in his eyes exactly what he had really wanted to do when he'd had her in his arms.

Her grandfather's gruff comment to him that he was worried about her had brought him here to Majorca, but ironically it was thanks to Nick Blayne that he was at last able to manoeuvre himself into a position of intimacy with her. Even if that intimacy was, for the moment, merely fictitious.

'Silas, you can't possibly really intend to marry Julia,' his mother had protested unhappily the night they had both attended Julia's eighteenth birthday.

'I take it you don't approve?' Silas had challenged her.

'Do you love her?' his mother had demanded, equally sharply.

'Sexual love is little more than an emotional virus, and in my opinion should not be used as the basis on which to build a relationship. I have thought for some time that Julia would be the perfect wife for me—once she has matured.'

'Silas…'

'I've made up my mind. After all, who could possibly be a better wife for me? She knows exactly what her duties would be once I inherit, both as a countess and as the mistress of Amberley. It will make the old boy happy— and tidy up a lot of loose ends. From a practical point of view, a marriage between us makes good sense. She's too young at the moment, of course. But I don't want to leave it too long.'

'Good sense? Silas, you're talking about marriage as though it's a…a business deal.'

'No, Mother, I'm merely being practical. As well as my responsibilities to Amberley, I've got to think of the Foundation as well. I don't want a wife who is going to change her mind and demand a huge divorce settlement. Julia has been born into a tradition of arranged marriages that goes way, way back. She understands these things.'

'Does she? My money is on her refusing you, Silas. Julia is a very feisty and passionate young woman. And an arranged marriage—that is so archaic!'

'They worked very well for hundreds of years, and they kept families and property together.'

His mother had sighed faintly and told him grimly, 'Sometimes you sound more like those dry dusty trustees you inherited from your father than a young man in his twenties. Don't you care that you will be depriving Julia as well as yourself of sharing your lives with someone you love?'

'Mother, love is merely an illusion—a delusion, in fact. A marriage built on mutual un-

derstanding and shared goals is far more practical, and far more likely to survive.'

'I doubt that Julia will agree with you. Look
at her!' his mother had demanded, and dutifully Silas had looked across at the short spiky
brown- and pink-striped head that had been all
he could see of her over her dance partner's
shoulder.

'Helen said that she came back from school
with her belly button pierced and talking about
having a tattoo—the family coat of arms, if
you please.'

That had been the year Julia had fallen passionately in love with the leader of a local an-
imal rights group, Silas remembered. The love
affair might have been short-lived, but the re-
sults of it were still very much in evidence.
The group, led by Julia, had defied her grandfather's gamekeeper and 'rescued' the young
pheasants he had been rearing, with the result
that one could not travel within ten miles of
Amberley now without encountering wandering cock pheasants.

It was also this relationship that had been
responsible for the five engaging greyhounds

Julia had 'rescued' and brought home and who now lived a life of luxury, having won her grandfather's heart via their shared misery at winter rheumatism and their love of a good whisky before bed.

Julia wasn't eighteen any more, though. And Silas had decided that it was time to put his plan into action. Julia's grandfather was growing frail, and Silas was very fond of him. It would mean a great deal to him to see his granddaughter married to his heir, Silas knew. Like him, the old Earl was also a very practical man—and what could be more practical than for his heir to marry his granddaughter, tying together the two remaining strands of the family and securing the future of Amberley at the same time?

It was very fortuitous that fate had decided to weigh in on his side and assist him in bringing his plans to fruition. Not that Silas considered that he needed to have fate on his side. He was perfectly capable of constructing his own good fortune.

The lift had finally stopped its sawing motion. Julia got out with relief, not sure whether to be appalled or triumphant when she realised that the 'penthouse suite' was actually in the rafters of the house, and that the tiny window in the corridor beside the lift was so low that an adult would have to kneel down in order to be able to look out of it.

She watched whilst Silas inserted the key into the lock of the heavy-looking door, and then opened it.

The room that lay beyond it was furnished as a sitting room, its double doors open to reveal the bedroom that lay beyond it. And a *huge* bed.

'Apparently there are two bathrooms,' she heard Silas informing her. 'And the sofa in the sitting room area converts to a double bed.'

'In case we want a foursome?' Julia couldn't resist saying lightly.

There was a cold steeliness in the look Silas lanced in her direction.

'The only kind of bed-sharing foursome I find acceptable is the non-sexual variety with a couple and their two children. And if Blayne's been dragging you down into that kind of gutter—'

Julia's face burned.

'It was just a joke, that's all. I didn't mean anything... I suppose you're expecting me to sleep on the sofa bed?'

'No. You can take the bed. After all, I'm not the one who has the problem waking up in the morning, am I?'

It was true that she was more of an owl than a lark, Julia knew, and it was also typical of Silas that he wouldn't have forgotten that as a teenager she had preferred to sleep late in the mornings—especially when she was on holiday.

'Which side of the bed do you prefer to sleep on?'

Julia gave him a suspicious look. 'If I've got the bed to myself it doesn't matter, does it?'

Silas exhaled slowly and warningly.

'Julia, it would help us both if you were able to refrain from looking for a sexual connotation in everything I say. My question about which side of the bed you prefer was provoked quite simply by a desire to know which of the two bathrooms it would make sense for you to use. That is to say, if you sleep on the left-hand side of the bed then, should you need the bathroom during the night, you would probably automatically use the one on the left. On the other hand—'

'All right, Professor, I get the picture.' Julia stopped him crossly. 'Why on earth couldn't you just say that, Silas?'

'Why couldn't you simply answer my question?'

'This is never going to work,' Julia told him, raking her hand impatiently through her hair.

'It certainly won't work if you don't want it to,' Silas agreed succinctly. 'If we want it to work then it's up to us both to make sure that it does.'

She certainly didn't want another run-in with Nick like the one she had had earlier in the evening, But his behaviour towards her had set her wondering just how he treated Lucy, and if in helping to preserve her marriage she was truly doing her friend a favour.

'There's no way I want to be the cause of Lucy being hurt,' she agreed. 'But if she's unhappy in the marriage too, then—'

'Has she told you that she's unhappy, or are you relying on Blayne for that piece of information?'

'I haven't discussed her marriage with Lucy, but—'

'But you have discussed it with her husband?' Silas pointed out coolly.

Julia slanted him a sideways and slightly wary glance. He was angry with her now; she could tell that just from the way in which his voice had hardened.

'This isn't the eighteen hundreds, Silas, when a woman couldn't speak to a friend's husband or have male friends.'

'It isn't your friendship that Blayne wants, though, is it?'

She was tired, and a small dull ache at the back of her eyes was steadily becoming an insistent stabbing pain. All she wanted to do was to have a bath and go to bed, not stand here arguing with Silas.

'Why don't you climb down off your moral high horse?' she suggested grittily. 'After all, you aren't in this just out of altruism, are you?'

'What do you mean?'

He went so still so quickly, like a hunter suddenly on the watch, that her own body tensed as well.

'I mean that aside from wanting to protect Gramps, there has to be something else in this for you.'

'Such as?'

'This woman you no longer want, for instance? The one you were happy to take to bed but don't want to get seriously involved with?'

'Like Blayne with you, you mean?'

He had relaxed again now, but he was still firing those poisoned darts, with deadly accuracy. Well, she could fire a few of her own.

Giving a small shrug, she told him, 'If you want to put yourself in the same category as Nick, then go ahead.'

She had known, of course, that he wouldn't like her comment, but she hadn't correctly calculated just how much.

When he took a step towards her she found that she was automatically stepping back, and, even more betrayingly, wrapping her arms around herself, her hands on her bruised flesh as though to protect it from further assault.

There was a look now in his eyes that she could not interpret—at least not with her brain. Her emotions were reacting to it with a sudden rush of hot miserable tears that burned the backs of her eyes.

'I can't understand what on earth you're even doing here in Majorca,' she burst out, exhausted. 'I suppose it must be something to do with the Foundation?'

There was the smallest of pauses before Silas agreed quietly, 'Yes.'

'Another acquisition, I suppose?' She was just too tired to argue now.

'In a manner of speaking. Although this one is very special...unique, in fact.'

'And worth the trouble this fake relationship with me is going to cause?' Julia asked him wryly.

'Well worth it,' Silas confirmed softly, before continuing, 'Now, which side of the bed?'

'The left. No, the right... I really don't mind. Which side do you prefer?' Julia asked him, and then went bright red. 'No, I didn't mean that. What I meant was, which *bathroom* would you prefer...?'

When he continued to look at her, she bit her lip, and then told him huskily, 'I can imagine what you're thinking, but I don't want to have sex with you, Silas.'

Just the lazy way in which he raised one eyebrow was enough to up her heart-rate.

'I wasn't aware that I had invited you to. But, if I had, why would you want to refuse me?'

'Why?' Julia took a deep breath and gave him an outraged look. 'Isn't it obvious? We don't mean anything to one another—we don't even like one another, never mind lust after each other. And even if we did... Well, it would just be too... Sex carries implications and...and responsibilities. And it's...' She was beginning to flounder and she knew it.

Before she could sink any further, Silas told her, 'You know, Jules, you are beginning to sound more and more like an anguished outdated virgin than the sexually experienced modern young woman I know you to be.'

'Well, I'm not,' she told him flatly. 'Not a virgin, I mean.'

'So why all the fuss and panic?'

Why indeed? She could hardly answer that question for herself without having to face certain previously unrecognised realities, never mind admit them to Silas.

Instead it was far easier and safer to take refuge in insouciance and say, as light-heartedly as she could manage, 'Maybe I was worried that my experience wouldn't match up to your own well-documented expertise. After all, that supermarket chain heiress you dated made it quite plain that she thought you were a real stud...and put that video of the two of you having sex on her website to prove it.'

'You watched it?'

'No! But I read about it in the papers.'

'That was three years ago, and since you never actually saw a face the man in the video could have been anyone. Still, I'm surprised by your attitude. I should have thought you'd have welcomed the opportunity to enjoy my so-called expertise and learn from it.'

Now what was she supposed to say?

Yes, please?

'Actually, we do have a client who runs, amongst other things, ''Learn to love your orgasm'' classes,' she told him truthfully.

'Learn to *what*?'

'You heard me. ''Learn to love your or-gasm'' classes. I suppose it means that you...you know...learn to feel comfortable about...erm... not being in control...'

'A sort of sexual female primal scream,' Silas offered, not quite straight-faced.

'It isn't funny,' Julia protested, but the gig-gles were already rising in her own throat and within seconds she was helpless with laughter herself.

That was the thing about Silas, she acknowl-edged later, as she luxuriated in a wonderfully deep bath, full of blissfully hot water, safe in the knowledge that the door to her bathroom was firmly locked. No matter how much he infuriated her, somehow he always had the knack of being able to make her laugh. She and Silas definitely shared a similar sense of humour.

Unlike Nick. Nick had never made her laugh. Nick's sense of humour involved being cruelly unkind to and about others.

Nick.

She looked at her upper arms where the flesh was already beginning to show the bruise marks he had left there.

CHAPTER FOUR

JULIA stretched luxuriously beneath the bed-clothes. She could smell coffee and she could hear voices. One of them a familiar voice. Silas's voice, she recognised, at virtually the same second as she realised *why* she was hearing it.

She opened her eyes and stared towards the now open double doors that led from the bedroom to the sitting room.

'Are you awake yet, sleepyhead?'

Silas himself appeared in the doorway, his legs bare beneath the hem of the robe he was wearing. He was holding a cup of coffee. Her mouth started to water. Coffee. She could live quite happily on a combination of caffeine and the buzz she got from her shoe habit. And this morning she was going to indulge that habit, having spent all week being tormented with longing for those impossible-to-resist little darlings she had heard about the day she had arrived.

'If you're waiting to shower and get dressed, don't let me stop you,' she informed Silas pointedly.

'I'd forgotten how grumpy you are when you wake up. Come and have a look at this view.'

And *she'd* forgotten how relentlessly and unnecessarily cheerful *he* was, Julia decided antagonistically.

'Shouldn't you put some clothes on?' she suggested.

'What for?'

What for? For her peace of mind, that was what! There was something seriously disturbing about having to cope with Silas wandering around in a bathrobe that was both too short and too small, so that it exposed a large amount of tanned, hair-roughened chest, in addition to somehow making it plain that those thighs it was just about covering were hugely powerful and very male. And surely he could have tied the belt a bit more securely, and put something on his feet. There was something distinctly sexual about a man's bare feet. In fact there was something distinctly sexual about Silas this morning, full-stop.

That familiar frisson of sensation she was feeling right now, which she had always previously put down to healthy antagonism, had somehow astonishingly morphed into a staggeringly acute sexual awareness of him. Beneath the bedclothes her nipples peaked with delight, ready and willing to show him the effect he was having on them, whilst the tension gripping her lower body made her wonder hollowly if she was on the point of losing her sanity.

How could she be lusting after Silas? She knew it had been a long time since she had last had sex, and it was true that she couldn't even remember the last time she had woken up to find a semi-naked man wandering around, but this semi-naked man was *Silas*, for heaven's sake. Silas, who had laughed out loud the first time he had seen her dressed up to go out on a date. Silas, who had threatened to 'beat her butt black and blue' when she had given the pheasants their freedom. Silas, who had threatened even worse violence to her person when he had found two of the greyhounds playing tug-of-war with his favourite Brooks Brothers shirt.

'I thought you'd prefer to have breakfast up here. So I've ordered you some coffee and juice, and I remembered that you like your eggs over easy.'

Coffee. Caffeine. That was what was wrong, Julia told herself feverishly. She was in caffeine shock. She had heard it could do weird things to you, but she hadn't realised just how weird.

'Are you sure you're wearing the right bathrobe?' she demanded. 'Only it doesn't seem to be your size.'

'Well, if you end up tripping over the hem of yours we'll have to swap. But until you get out of that bed we aren't going to know, are we?'

'I can't get out of bed with you standing there.'

'You can't? Why not? Worried about the effect the Mickey Mouse PJs might have on me?'

'That was when I was ten,' Julia told him awfully.

'So was the teddy bear hot water bottle, but last time I visited the old guy there it was, hanging up along with the others.'

Muttering at him, Julia mentally cursed herself for getting into bed naked in the first place. It would serve Silas right if she just clean got out of bed starkers. Mickey Mouse PJs indeed. Huh. That would show him.

After all, it wasn't as though no man had ever seen her naked. Several had, even if right now she could not remember ever having felt this hot-shot tingle of fizzing, trepidation-coated excitement before.

'Your eggs will be cold,' Silas warned her.

That was all he knew, Julia decided feverishly. Right now her 'eggs' were feeling pretty hot, and ready for the kind of action that led to one and one becoming three. Or maybe even four, if they had twins. She had always thought twins must be fun...

She gave a small yelp of protest against her own thoughts and hurriedly got out of bed, forgetting her nudity in her eagerness to escape from the images inside her head of two adorable dark-haired babies with Silas's ice-blue eyes.

'What happened to the tattoo?'

She was very careful not to turn round, but instead to look back over her shoulder as she stood sheltering behind the half-open bathroom door.

'What tattoo?'

'The family coat of arms. Mother said you'd had it tattooed across your butt.'

'I did—for a dare. But it wasn't permanent. Anything else you want to know?'

'No, not right now. I guess it tells a guy quite a bit about a woman when he can see that she doesn't sunbathe in the nude.'

'Haven't you heard of sun damage?' Julia retorted smartly. 'If I want an all-over tan I have it sprayed on.'

'Take it from me, the cute white triangles are much more of a turn-on. Any guy would feel good knowing he was getting to see something the world at large hadn't had access to. I'd forgotten how small you are without those ridiculous shoes you insist on wearing.'

'Small?' Julia stepped angrily towards him and then shot back, her face pink. 'I'm five foot five.'

'Like I said, I'd forgotten how small you are,' Silas drawled.

'Well, I haven't forgotten what an arrogant, know-it-all you are,' Julia snapped back at him crossly, before disappearing into her bathroom and firmly closing the door.

To her own disgust she was actually trembling slightly, with a mixture of rage and emotional frustration. How could she have forgotten just how much and how easily Silas had always managed to infuriate her, with that lordly belief of his that everything he said and did was both superior and right?

What must it be like to be so impervious and invulnerable? The problem with Silas was that he had never suffered. But whilst wealth and position had protected him from financial hardship and the rigours of modern-day life, it was surely his nature that had ensured he was impervious to emotional vulnerability and self-doubt. No one had ever successfully challenged his beliefs or made him question them.

No one had ever made him doubt himself or what motivated him. Even that wise gentleman her grandfather treated him with respect and deference.

But she wasn't going to do so! What she wouldn't give to be around on the day when Silas discovered what it felt like to be human and hurt, Julia decided savagely as she showered and dried.

She pulled on her own waiting bathrobe, which of course was not oversized and meant for a man, but instead exactly the same as the one Silas was wearing.

Of course it was oversized on her, but the fact that it wrapped round her with fabric to spare and reached the floor was not, in her present mood, a disadvantage.

She found Silas standing beside the open windows of the sitting room, drinking his coffee.

'There's a balcony out there, but I'm not sure how safe it is,' he warned her. 'Want some coffee?'

'I'll pour my own, thanks,' Julia told him sharply.

'I'd eat your eggs first.'

'I don't eat eggs any more.'

It wasn't the truth, but it was well worth depriving herself of them to have the joy of rejecting his authority.

But of course Silas wasn't so easily out-maneuvered.

'No wonder you look thin,' he told her disparagingly.

'I am not thin!'

'What's on the agenda for today?'

'Nothing much, really. The Famous Couple and their people are flying out this afternoon, and presumably, Dorland will be going to see them off safely. But we aren't involved in that. Lucy and Nick are due to return to England tonight, and, like I said, I'm booked on a flight for Naples.'

'So that leaves you with a free morning?'

Julia hesitated. She had no intention of handing Silas the opportunity to further deride her by informing him that she intended to spend her free morning indulging in her shoe habit. Why should she, when even her closest friends shook their heads over it so much that secretly she did sometimes feel guilty?

'Not exactly. I've got a few errands to run, some laundry to collect, and I want to go to the bank—that kind of thing.'

'Fine. I'll come with you. It will give me an opportunity to look round the old part of the town.'

'No! I mean, there's no need for you to come with me. You'd only be bored. I've got some paperwork to catch up on as well, and some phone calls to make.'

'I see.'

Did she really think that he couldn't work out that she was planning to see Blayne? Silas wondered cynically.

If it hadn't been for the fact that he knew the other man was flying back to the UK later in the day, whilst *he* was accompanying Julia to Italy, he might have been inclined to do something about it, but he could see no sense in pushing her into doing something stupid like running off with Blayne.

It was a pity that she hadn't remained at Amberley after leaving school, riding her horse, doing good works and keeping her grandfather company while she matured enough for him to marry her. He had not been too concerned about her involvement with Prêt a Party because it had freed up time he was able to put to good use in focusing on streamlining the operation of the Foundation.

Now, however, things were different. Now he was ready to put into operation his decision to make her his wife. She was, after all, in so many ways the perfect wife for him. They shared a common history, but their blood tie was not too close. She had virtually been brought up at Amberley, as had her mother, and would have no problem fitting in or running it. Julia, via her family history, understood the duties of a marriage such as theirs. Her grandfather would naturally approve of their union, and, whilst there was no obligation on him to submit his marriage for the older man's approval, life would be easier all round if he did approve of the woman who would one day run his beloved home.

Not that Silas had any intention of basing himself permanently at Amberley. He was an

American, after all, with responsibilities and duties to fulfil to the Foundation established by his own grandfather. Julia, he felt sure, would make an admirable wife in that respect, especially with his formidable mother to guide her. Their children—and there would be children—would grow up in a secure emotional environment, because there would be no divorce. He had already decided that after the birth of their first child he would commission Julia's portrait, with her wearing the Maharajah's gift, just like her ancestor.

Naturally, Silas was aware that many people—Julia included—would not appreciate his unemotional and practical view on marriage, but a man who was responsible for ensuring that billions of dollars and an earldom were passed intact down through the generations could not afford the folly of being governed by his emotions.

But now, like a small flaw in the middle of an otherwise perfect diamond, there was Nick Blayne. It was Silas's belief that a person made his own luck, but he was forced to admit that it had been a bonus in his favour to be in a position to drive a wedge between Nick and Julia and at the same time take advantage of Julia's loyalty to her friend by proposing their own fake relationship.

He certainly wasn't prepared to have all his plans disrupted by the inconvenience of Julia getting involved in a messy divorce.

He wasn't going to press the issue now, though. Blayne would be going back to London with his wife, whilst he intended to make sure that when Julia returned to the UK it would be in order to prepare for their marriage. And he had from now until the end of the year to achieve his goal.

True, there was the irksome and irritating problem of a certain spoiled American heiress who was declaring to anyone who would listen to her, without any encouragement from him, that she was passionately in love with him. It was no secret in old money New York society that there was more than a suspicion of mental instability in her family tree, but Silas had grown impatient of her dramatic and over-emotional behaviour. It wasn't even as though he had actually dated her—although she

seemed to think that the fact that she contin-
ually stalked him, turning up uninvited at
events she knew he was attending, constituted
some kind of relationship. If she had known
the first thing about him she would have
known that she was wasting her time, and that
by sending him a video of herself having sex
with two well-endowed musclemen would not
tempt him to fall in love with her, as she had
repeatedly insisted she knew he would. Silas
had no intention of doing anything so imprac-
tical as falling in love with anyone.

Still, a beneficial side effect of the announcement of his engagement to Julia was
that it would, thankfully, bring Aimee to her
senses—or at least what senses she possessed,
Silas decided unkindly.

She had managed to leave the hotel without
anyone stopping her to ask where she was going, and Julia could feel her heart starting to
beat that familiar little bit faster as she turned
into the alleyway that led to the shoe shop.

She stopped guiltily to look back over her
shoulder. Of course she should feel ashamed
of herself, and no doubt she would later, but

right now all she could think of were the shoes. And there they were, in the window, with their darling high delicate heels, and the kind of low-cut front that she knew would show just the right amount of toe cleavage.

She could stand here all day and look at them. But if she did that someone else might buy them, and she couldn't bear that. Hurriedly she pushed open the shop door.

Over an hour later she left the shop, clutching two carrier bags, her face flushed and pink with happiness and her eyes shining. It had been so impossible to choose between the two pairs of shoes she had fallen for that in the end she had decided she had to have both. They had been just too beautiful to resist.

'No Nick, Lucy?' Silas enquired, putting down the newspaper he had been reading as Lucy walked into the pleasantly shaded patio area at the back of the hotel.

'No, he had to go into town to attend to a few things. He must have his mobile switched off as well, because I've just tried to ring him.'

Her innocent statement confirmed his own suspicions, and it was on the tip of Silas's tongue to suggest cynically that she try Julia's instead.

'I hope he gets back soon. Dorland has just been on the telephone to say that there's a big panic on at the villa. Apparently, the Tiffany necklace has gone missing.'

'Don't tell me he's surprised?'

When Lucy looked puzzled, Silas explained, 'Martina is known for her acquisitive nature, and it won't be the first time she's held on to a piece of loaned jewellery and refused to hand it back.'

'But Dorland will have to pay Tiffany for it. Because they loaned it to *him*,' Lucy protested, looking shocked.

'I doubt the odd million or so would make much of a dent in Dorland's bank account, and in fact I wouldn't be surprised if the whole thing wasn't some kind of publicity stunt. My guess is that Dorland will have informed the media first, and not the police.'

'Silas, you are far too cynical,' Lucy told him gently.

'It isn't cynicism, it's common sense,' Silas corrected her, glancing at his watch and then putting down his paper. 'Julia went into town earlier—she should be on her way back by now. I think I'll take a walk and see if I can spot her.'

'Julia's gone in to town?' Lucy's forehead crinkled into a small frown. 'Oh, I thought she said last night that she intended to spend the morning with you?'

'She'd probably forgotten then about the laundry she had to pick up.'

It wasn't his business to protect Lucy Blayne's feelings, Silas reminded himself, but the poor girl was so obviously vulnerable— and besides, it wouldn't serve his purpose to create suspicion and mistrust between Julia and her best friend.

She really didn't know which pair of shoes were her favourite, Julia mused dreamily as she sauntered back to the hotel. True, the pair she had seen in the shop window had been her first love, and she had had to have them, but then the assistant had shown her the other pair, and a pang of such acute longing had gripped her that she had just not been able to choose between them. Thank heavens she had had the good sense to buy both pairs.

'Hello, Jules.'

She came to an abrupt and wary halt as the alleyway opened up into a small square and Nick materialised in front of her. The square was quiet and empty, apart from two old men sitting outside a small café, both of whom looked as though they were asleep.

'I'm just on my way back to the hotel,' Julia announced, trying to assure herself that if she acted as though Nick's aggressive attack on her had not actually taken place then somehow that would require him to behave decently.

'Well, well,' Nick murmured. 'Look who's here.'

Julia gave a small gasp of dismay as she looked across the square and saw Silas walking purposefully towards them.

'Let's see how he likes looking at this, shall we?'

Before she could stop him Nick had pushed her back against the wall and was kissing her with mock passion, as she fought to break free of him.

He didn't release her until Silas's shadow was falling across her face, and kept his back to Silas before he turned to saunter triumphantly away, so that only she could see the cruel satisfaction in his eyes.

'It wasn't like it seemed—' she began shakily, as Silas stood in front of her, blotting out the warmth of the sun so that she felt so chilled she actually started to shiver.

'Do you remember what I threatened to do when you set those wretched pheasants free?' Silas asked her, almost gently.

Julia was not deceived; she had heard that dulcet note in his voice before and knew exactly what it meant.

'Yes, you said if I ever did anything like that again I'd feel the flat of your hand on my butt, good and hard. You couldn't get away with threatening me like that now. It's illegal to smack a child.'

'But you aren't a child; you are an adult— even if you don't seem to possess the ability to reason like one. And right now the best way, in fact the only way I can think of letting you know how furious you have made me, would be for me to apply the weight of my hand to that pretty little *derrière* of yours, until it blushes pink with shame for you.

'Can't you see what you're doing? You said that you didn't want to hurt Lucy, and yet you lied to me and to her so that you could sneak out and meet up with her husband. What if she had been the one to see Blayne pushing you against that wall as though he were about to take you right there and then?'

There was no gentleness left in his voice now, and Julia quailed beneath the savage lash of its anger.

She was no weak-willed pushover, though, to be treated like a child and threatened with the kind of humiliation Silas had just described.

'I did not sneak out to meet Nick! I'd only just bumped into him. He kissed me like that deliberately, because he had seen you. He's angry because I've told him I won't sleep with him, and now he wants to hurt me and get at you as well!'

Her voice was trembling slightly with both indignation at Silas's accusation and reaction to her own mental image of his open palm, spanking teasingly and sexily down on her bare behind whilst she tried to squirm free. She couldn't help feeling a little bit turned on both by the image and her own reaction to it. There was something definitely rather naughtily delicious about the thought of such teasing love-play. Not that she was into anything as potentially painful as true S and M, but a little gentle game of forfeits with the kind of 'punishment' that would involve her partner indulging in some pretend bottom-spanking could be fun if she was in the right mood. And with the right man... A man like Silas?

Julia could feel herself starting to blush a little at the inner excitement caused by her own thoughts, but Silas soon brought her back to reality, insisting, 'You claim you met Blayne by chance, and yet it was obvious to me this morning, when you said you intended to go into town, that you were hiding something.'

'But it wasn't a secret meeting with Nick,' Julia protested.

'Then what was it?' Silas challenged her.

Julia looked down at the bags Nick had made her drop.

'Shoes,' she muttered guiltily.

'Shoes?'

Silas looked from the carrier bags to her flushed face and then back again.

'You didn't want me to know you intended to buy *shoes*?' he questioned, bemused.

Julia could only shake her head. If Silas didn't know about her shoe addiction then she certainly wasn't going to expose herself to his mockery by telling him.

'Come on, we'd better get back to the hotel,' he announced, reaching down to pick up her bags.

Immediately Julia tried to stop him, not wanting to allow her precious purchases out of her own control.

'Julia, I'll carry them for you,' Silas insisted, taking hold of her arm to hold her back so that he could pick them up, but he was gripping her arm exactly where Nick had bruised it the previous evening, and Julia couldn't stop herself from giving a small, agonised gasp of pain.

'What...?'

The sleeves of her tee shirt just about covered the bruise marks—or at least they did until Silas pushed one of them up to reveal them.

'Who did this?' he demanded quietly.

Julia didn't even think of trying to lie.

'Nick,' she told him shakily. 'Last night. He was furious when I told him about you...'

'So he did this to you?'

The surge of angry protectiveness that gripped him caught him off guard. Of course no man should hurt a woman, but he was not used to experiencing such intense or possessive emotions.

He looked across the square in the direction Nick had taken.

Julia put a restraining hand on his arm. 'I don't think he meant to hurt me, Silas.'

'But he did. Your arms are black and blue—'

Julia started to laugh.

'What's so funny?' Silas demanded.

Mischievously, Julia reminded him, 'As my bottom deserved to be, according to you.'

Silas looked at her. Her lips were parted and her face was flushed. There was a look in her eyes that told him...

He put down the carriers and said softly, 'Something tells me that you find the prospect of a little spanking rather erotic.'

Julia laughed and looked away demurely. 'You're the one who keeps threatening to punish me,' she told him breathlessly.

Heavens, she couldn't really be flirting like this with *Silas*, could she?

'Mmm, but you're the one who keeps reminding me that I haven't carried out my threat as yet,' Silas murmured. 'And the one who keeps on provoking me...'

'Provoking you?'

'You certainly provoked me this morning, with that cute, peachy little butt of yours.'

Now it wasn't just her flirting with Silas. He was flirting right back. And the heady excitement of what they were doing was irresistible.

'You said I was thin,' Julia pouted.

'I guess maybe I didn't make a close enough appraisal.'

He was actually moving closer to her and reaching behind her, and—oh, lordy—he was sliding his hand right down her back and cupping—no, caressing—one firm buttock. Helplessly Julia leaned into him, even her shoes forgotten.

This was definitely *not* part of his game plan, Silas recognised as he looked down at her closed eyes and parted lips. He wanted his—their—kids to be conceived after they were married, not before.

He bent his head and kissed her briefly, ignoring the look of disappointment in her eyes when she opened them as he released her.

'We'd better get back. I saw Lucy at the hotel, and apparently Dorland's in a sweat because the necklace he had on loan from Tiffany has gone missing.'

'Oh, no! Poor Dorland. Maybe they'll have found it by now,' Julia suggested, as Silas picked up her bags. 'Stuff like that happens all the time. These big stars have such a huge retinue that no one ever seems to know what anyone else is doing. One of the PRs has probably put the necklace somewhere safe.'

She was growing more sexually attracted to Silas by the hour, Julia admitted to herself— or had the attraction always been there without her wanting to recognise it?

'Oh, there you are. Nick's gone over to the villa to see if he can be of any help to Dorland,' Lucy began as they walked into the hotel, only to look accusingly at Julia's carrier bags before exclaiming, 'Jules—not more shoes!'

'I had to have them.'

'How often have I heard that before? You do realise, I hope, Silas, that Jules has a very serious shoe habit?'

'Lucy, wait until you see them. They've got the perfect toe cleavage shape,' Julia burst out enthusiastically. 'And the heels—they had one pair with the cutest little kittens, and another with serious stilettos…and…'

'You had to buy them both!'

Julia hung her head.

'No wonder you snuck out this morning without telling me where you were going,' Lucy accused her. 'You're going to have to find a way of restraining her, Silas,' Lucy warned him, mock seriously.

'Yes, I think I am,' Silas agreed gravely, but when Julia looked across at him the wicked glint in his eyes told her that the kind of restraint *he* was envisaging, had nothing whatsoever to do with preventing her from buying shoes.

What in the world was happening to her? She didn't really know—but she certainly knew what she would like to happen, Julia admitted ruefully as she looked discreetly but very interestedly at the tell tale bulge that no amount of expensive tailoring could completely hide.

Sex with Silas. Mmm…

'Jules, will you please stop looking at Silas like that? You're embarrassing me.' Lucy laughed.

'So, tell me some more about this shoe fetish thing you've got.'

It was after lunch and Lucy and Nick had gone upstairs to pack, and Julia and Silas were still sitting outside, finishing the bottle of wine

Silas had bought to go with the alfresco lunch they had eaten in the small hotel courtyard.

'It isn't a fetish. It's just that I can't help wanting to buy shoes.'

'Uh-huh. And toe cleavage? What exactly is that?'

Honestly—men. They didn't know anything! Julia shook her head and explained in a kind voice, 'It's when the front of your shoe shows a bit of your toes, and it's seriously sexy.'

'Show me?'

'I can't—not properly anyway—because I'm not wearing the right kind of shoes,' Julia told him. 'You'll see what I mean when I wear them.'

'I can't wait.'

'I'd better go up and pack. We need to leave for the airport for our flight to Naples at five.' Would he offer to come with her? And if he did...

'I've got a few phone calls to make.'

Julia tried not to feel disappointed.

'And, by the way, I've cancelled your booking at that guest house and booked us both into the Hotel Arcadia instead.'

'The Arcadia? But that's the most exclusive hotel in Positano. It costs the earth to stay there, and Lucy—'

'Stop panicking. Naturally I shall be paying the bill. Did Lucy say that Dorland was going to come over?'

'Yes. About three.'

Upstairs in the suite, Julia packed quickly and efficiently—leaving plenty of room for her new shoes. Her normal travelling work 'uniform' consisted of her current favourite pair of jeans, (her love affair with jeans came a close second to her shoe addiction—Julia was simply not what she called a 'suit and two veg' fan), several tee shirts and strappy tops, a swimsuit just in case she got the chance to have a lazy day, and a long, sleek, very plain jersey dress that rolled up into a ball, which she wore when she needed to be dressed up. Added to these basics were casual cut-offs and a few boho-type tops, plus a much loved floaty skirt.

Julia adored accessorising her clothes with one and sometimes more of her trademark boho 'finds'. Her personal look was very different from the designer 'footballer's wife' style adopted by so many of their clients. One of her most cherished moments was the time a stylist for *Sex and the City* had stopped her in the street to ask where she had got the top she had been wearing. Julia's current favourite accessory was a dark brown wide leather belt, ornamented with leather flower petals sewn with tiny turquoise beads to form the flower stamens. She had bought it from a stall at Camden Market, and wore it at every opportunity. She had been seriously tempted to buy a pair of Aztec-inspired turquoise earrings she had also seen on the stall, but had managed to resist.

Her packing finished, she looked at her watch—the plain but oh, so elegant Cartier that Lucy had so generously insisted on buying for all three of them out of her first profits.

Those had been happy, heady days, filled with fun and laughter. Julia frowned. The initial success of the business seemed to have been replaced by a series of financial problems, causing poor Lucy to have to dig deep into her trust fund to provide Prêt a Party with

more capital. No wonder her friend was looking so stressed.

It was almost three o'clock. She might as
well go back down and wait for Dorland to
arrive. Most of the necessary organisation for
his end-of-summer party had already been
done by Dorland himself, but, as Julia knew,
he liked to fuss and fret over every tiny little
detail, and virtually every day she received
anxious urgent e-mails from him.

She had just stepped out of the lift into the
guest house's dusty, faded hallway when her
mobile rang.

'Darling!' She heard her mother's voice exclaiming. 'How naughty of you not to tell us
about you and Silas. I couldn't believe it at
first when Mrs. Williams showed me the article about the two of you in that celebrity gossip magazine she buys. Such a lovely photograph of the two of you, darling, but I must
admit I was rather shocked. Not that we aren't
all thrilled. We are, of course—especially
Daddy. I drove straight round to see him, and
he was so pleased that he instructed Bowers to
open a bottle of the wine he put down when

you were born, to celebrate. It's what he's always longed for. Of course I had to ring Nancy. So silly of me to get the time difference wrong, but naturally she is as excited as we are. You'll be married at Amberley, of course—every Amberley bride always is, but have you decided on a date yet? I do so think that winter weddings have a certain *élan.*'

With every excited word her mother spoke, Julia's insides churned a little bit more tensely.

'Ma…' She tried to protest when she could eventually interrupt her excited happiness, but it was no use. Her mother, as high as a kite on maternal delight, was too busy listing all the many sections of the family who would want to supply a potential bridesmaid.

Silas was on his own in the small courtyard. Julia didn't waste any time announcing in despair, 'Ma's just been on the phone. She thinks we're getting married.'

When Silas refused to react with the shock she had expected, she added, 'She's told your mother, and Gramps was so pleased he instructed Bowers to open a bottle of the wine he put down when I was born.'

'The Château d'Yquem, eh?' Silas looked impressed. 'He's obviously pleased, then.'

'What? Of course he's pleased. According to Ma it's what he's always wanted. But that isn't the point. We *aren't* engaged—we aren't even in a *relationship*. Can you imagine what it's going to do to him when he finds out the truth?'

'You're right,' Silas agreed firmly. 'We can't let that happen.'

Julia had the unnerving feeling that she was a passenger in a car that had suddenly taken a dangerous curve at high speed and left the road completely.

'Silas…'

'For his sake we're just going to have to go along with the situation for now.'

'Go along with it? Ma's already planning the wedding—right down to the number of bridesmaids!'

'Mothers are like that,' Silas agreed gravely.

Julia glared at him.

'You aren't taking this seriously,' she accused him.

'Because it isn't serious,' Silas told her. 'Okay, it's unfortunate, but it's hardly the end of the world. People get engaged to one another every day.'

'Yes, but *they* have a reason for being engaged,' Julia told him through gritted teeth. 'We don't.'

'No, but we do have a reason to maintain the fiction that we are engaged.'

'Gramps?' she guessed helplessly.

'Exactly,' Silas agreed. 'No matter what our personal feelings—or lack of them—I am sure we are both agreed that not upsetting your grandfather is of more importance than they are.'

'Yes, of course,' Julia agreed immediately.

'So, then, we are both agreed that for his sake there is nothing we can do other than to accept that we are now ''engaged''.'

Julia swallowed—hard. 'But ultimately…'

'Ultimately a solution will have to be found,' Silas agreed calmly. 'Either by us or perhaps by life itself.'

Julia looked at him. 'You mean that Gramps might…that he may not… I know his heart isn't very strong, but—'

Before she could continue, the door to the courtyard opened and Dorland hurried in.

'I suppose you've heard about those wretched diamonds? How on earth can they be lost? Martina swears she remembers taking them off and putting them back in their case, and asking someone to give them to the bloody security guard—who I paid a small fortune to do nothing other than watch over them. He says he never got them, Martina can't remember who she gave them to, and she screams every time I try to get her to remember. And George—would you believe it?—was shagging one of the waitresses when Martina took them off. I've got Tiffany on the phone every five minutes, demanding that I pay them a million dollars for their necklace. Thank goodness I managed to persuade the *Beast* to pay for an exclusive account of how George was discovered *in flagrante*, the very night he had reaffirmed his marriage vows. You should see the photograph they've done—George and this girl, naked apart from a diamond necklace.'

'The *Beast*?' Silas questioned.

'Dorland's pet name for a certain red-top daily,' Julia explained.

'My little joke, Silas.' Dorland beamed. 'The editor, the dearest boy, has a fondness for dressing up as King Kong, as part of his mating ritual.'

'Dorland, I've got a bone to pick with you,' Julia informed him grimly.

'Oh?'

'My mother's daily showed her an article in *A-List Life* with photographs of me and Silas and the information that—'

'I'm sorry, sweetheart, but I just couldn't resist.' Dorland stopped her, looking more smug than repentant. 'It was such a tempting tidbit. Fortunately the photographs I told the guys to take of the two of you turned out well, and I told Murray to make room for them. I thought up the headline myself. ''Keeping it in the Family.'' Then it said, ''My spies tell me that one of *A-List*'s favourite party girls is soon to be planning a wedding. And guess who to? Her grandfather, the Earl of Amberley, is bound to be pleased, since her husband-to-be is also his heir, the American billionaire Silas

Cabot Carter.'' You'll be getting married at Amberley of course?' he continued, unconsciously echoing Julia's mother.

'Of course,' Silas agreed smoothly. 'But not yet. I haven't forgotten my promise to Lucy.' Really, Silas reflected inwardly, things couldn't have begun to work out better if he had planned them this way himself.

'Jules, I've been thinking—the fireworks. Do you really think it's a good idea to colour-co-ordinate them?' Dorland demanded, having obviously lost interest in their 'engagement'.

'I think it's an excellent idea,' Julia assured him, well aware how much it would cost if she were to instruct the firework suppliers to change the order she had already given them.

'Lucy, I know you're about to leave, but have you got a minute?'

'Of course. Nick's gone down with our stuff to wait for the taxi.'

She hated doing this, Julia thought. No way did she want to lie to her best friend, but with her grandfather having sent off a notice of her supposed engagement to *The Times*, Lucy was bound to wonder why on earth she hadn't said something.

'Silas and I are getting engaged.'

'Jules!' Immediately Lucy threw her arms around her and hugged her fiercely, her face alight with happiness. 'Oh, I am so pleased for you. You're perfect for one another. Oh, Jules, how exciting—and you never said a word...'

'It's all been very sudden,' Julia told her uncomfortably. Well, that much at least was true.

Despite the fact that her friend was obviously happy with the news, Lucy looked weary.

'You're happy, aren't you, Lucy?' Julia demanded abruptly. 'I mean, with Nick?'

'Of course I am,' Lucy told her immediately. 'Why shouldn't I be?'

'A word with you, if you please, Blayne,' Silas demanded quietly.

This was the first time he had managed to catch Nick on his own following Julia's revelations.

Nick shrugged. 'Sure. How can I help?'

Silas studied him assessingly. Was it only another man who could see that the too-handsome face hinted at weakness?

'You're walking a very precarious line right now, and whilst your marriage is not my concern, Julia's well-being is.'

'You're warning me off?' Nick asked lightly, smiling. He gave another small shrug. 'Jules has a very passionate nature. She's never made any secret of the fact that she has a bit of a thing for me—'

'Really? And what do you have a thing for, Blayne? Apart from assaulting women, of course.'

An angry red tide of colour had begun to seep up under Nick's tan.

'I don't know what she told you, but she was—'

'Trying to tell you that she wasn't interested in having sex with you. Let me give you a friendly warning. You've been lucky. You married Lucy. Don't push that luck too far, otherwise you could very easily find yourself unmarried to her. Right now she's all that's stopping me from turning your life inside out.

You're scum—you know that, and I know that. So, in case you want what we both know to become public knowledge, I suggest that in future you remember what a very lucky man you are.'

'It's all very well for you, standing there all high and mighty with your billions of dollars behind you,' Nick burst out savagely. 'You don't even begin to know what the real world is all about. If you did—'

'If I did, I still wouldn't use a woman to satisfy my own needs if that wasn't what she wanted. Money has nothing to do with morals, Blayne. We've all got freedom of choice.'

'Bastard,' Silas heard Nick mutter venomously as he walked away from him. But the sudden compression of his mouth into a hard line wasn't caused by Nick's aggression.

He had claimed a moral superiority over Blayne, and it was true that he would never physically abuse or force a woman in any kind of way, but according to his mother in planning to marry Julia he was using her.

'A marriage between us will benefit her as much as it will me,' he had told her.

'Only if she shares your thinking, Silas, and I have to say that I don't think she will. You claim to be a practical man who has no desire for a marriage based on love. I doubt that Julia will share that point of view.'

Silas stopped himself. This was hardly the best time for him to start indulging in a guilt trip over Julia's feelings.

Any practical person would agree with him that a marriage between them would be extremely beneficial to both of them. In and out of bed. He considered himself to be an aware and fair lover, and Julia hadn't flirted with him earlier on because she *didn't* want to have sex with him, had she? There was no reason why they shouldn't share a mutually very satisfying sex life. If they did, then he was certainly prepared to remain a faithful husband, and he felt confident that he could keep Julia satisfied enough not to want to stray herself. Their marriage would certainly have a far stronger foundation than one based on 'romantic love'. One only had to look at the tragedy of Lucy's marriage to Blayne to know that.

CHAPTER FIVE

THERE were undeniably some advantages to her 'engagement' to Silas, Julia reflected as their chauffeur-driven limousine swept them down toward Positano, and first-class travel had to be at the top of the list.

Julia knew that many people found Silas dauntingly formidable. His unemotional practicality had certainly irked her over the years, but there were times when a practical man was a bonus and this was definitely one of them. She considered herself to be a modern, independent woman, but she had certainly enjoyed having nothing to do other than sit back and relax and admire the awe-inspiring Amalfi coastline.

Silas, predictably, had been working, his BlackBerry handheld PDA device in constant use as he phoned and e-mailed, while the chauffeur with true Italian *élan* and a breathtakingly macho disregard for the coaches lumbering the other way.

'Relax,' Silas had murmured at one point, when she had audibly drawn in her breath, sure that they would go over the cliff. 'He knows he won't get a tip if we don't survive.'

It had astonished her that he had noticed her apprehension. He certainly hadn't been looking at her. She knew that, because every time she had looked at him he had been totally focused on e-mailing.

What would it take to shake Silas out of that cool, distancing manner of his and into the heat of raw human passion…or rather who would it take? She would certainly need to be a very strong woman, and a very determined one. What would he be like as a lover? Experienced, certainly, and knowledgeable about what pleased a woman for sure. Silas set high standards for himself, and his skills. And a woman would be able to trust him to take care of everything there was to be taken care of. Silas would have a clean bill of health and an awareness of what could be safely risked and what could not. He would take due care to make sure that his lover experienced the maximum amount of pleasure without inflicting on her any kind of pain.

Physically, perhaps, but what about emotionally? Was Silas, with his cool distance from the rest of the human race and their untidy emotions, capable of understanding what it meant to be hurt emotionally?

'I've e-mailed your grandfather, apologising for not asking his formal permission for our engagement. I told him that your impetuosity overwhelmed us.'

'*My* impetuosity?' Julia challenged him.

Silas smiled at her.

'Well, he would hardly be likely to believe me if I said it was mine, would he?' I've also e-mailed my mother, and the New York society columns.'

'Have you told her that my impetuosity is to blame as well?' Julia asked wryly.

'My mother doesn't need an explanation.'

Whilst Julia was silently digesting his comment, Silas added, 'You're going to need an engagement ring, but, I've suggested to your grandfather we wait until you can return to New York with me.'

'Silas, I don't want a ring.'

She might just as well not have spoken.

'It seems appropriate to me that you should wear the Monckford diamond.'

'What?' Julia stared at him. 'You mean the one the Sixth Earl fought that duel over?'

'Actually, it was his wife's honour over which he fought the duel, but since it was the fact that she was foolish enough to be wearing the ring when she went to meet her lover, yes, I do mean that one. Traditionally it was the family betrothal ring, so it seems fitting that you should wear it now.'

Julia took refuge from her own chaotic thoughts by saying crossly, 'I thought you were supposed to run the Foundation, not spend your time trying to repossess every bauble the family ever owned.'

'The Monckford Diamond is hardly a bauble. In fact, it is an extremely rare and historic stone.'

'Thank heavens I don't have to wear it permanently. If it looks anything like it does in the Countess's portrait, it must be incredibly ugly,' Julia could not resist saying disparagingly.

Silas had always incited her to this kind of angry tit for tat, as though somehow they both had to try and outdo one another. But, no matter how much she goaded him, Silas never reacted with a satisfactory show of emotion.

They had reached Positano, its rows of pastel-washed buildings clinging to the steep hillside whilst the Mediterranean lay blue and calm below them.

No wonder artists and poets had fallen in love with this place, Julia reflected as she gazed out of the car widow in silent appreciation. And no wonder too that the Silverwoods had wanted to come here, to the place where they had first met, to celebrate two such special family events.

As regular visitors to Positano, the Silverwoods had a favourite hotel where they always stayed, and Julia had managed, after some incredibly difficult negotiations, to ensure that they would have the exclusive use of a private dining room there, that opened out onto a terrace overlooking the sea, for the celebratory meal. Not unnaturally, the manager of the hotel had demanded a large fee for the use of both dining room and patio, at what was virtually the height of the summer season.

Privately Julia was not sure she would have chosen such an exclusive and expensive venue for the celebration of an eighteenth birthday, and during initial discussions she had recognised that the Silverwoods' teenage son was not as excited about the prospect of the double celebration as his parents. Diplomatically she had suggested to her clients that they might think about throwing a more robust type of event exclusively for their son, so that he could celebrate his coming of age with his friends.

The car turned in to the entrance to the Arcadia hotel, past the discreet plaque that bore the legend 'Leading Hotels of the World'. She already knew that the Arcadia had been built in the eighteenth century as a private villa, and had been opened as a hotel in the early 1950s. Its rooms were apparently still furnished as though it were a private home, with carefully chosen antiques and *objets d'art*, and certainly the reception area bore out this description.

They were shown almost immediately to their suite, and Julia caught her breath as she saw the views from the windows. The hotel must surely command some of the best views in Positano, Julia decided as Silas tipped the porter.

'This is heavenly,' she murmured appreciatively, unable to take her eyes off the sparkling blue of the Mediterranean.

'What's the plan of action for tomorrow?' Silas asked, merely glancing briefly at the view as he reached for his BlackBerry.

'The family will have already arrived today, and by tonight so will most of the guests. For tomorrow, we've organised the hire of a private yacht that will take everyone to Capri, where they will have lunch. Then tomorrow evening there will be a champagne reception at the hotel. Some of the guests won't make it in time for the Capri trip, so the following day those who wish to do so can go to Amalfi. For those who don't, a buffet lunch will be provided at the hotel, with the main event—the formal dinner—taking place that evening.'

'And that's it?' Silas asked her.

'That's it,' Julia agreed, straight-faced. 'Except, of course, for the flowers, and the hairdresser, and the food, and of course the wine, plus getting the presents here, et cetera, et cetera.'

He had put down his BlackBerry and come to study the view. There wasn't very much room on the small balcony, which meant that he had to stand behind her, so close that she could feel the heat coming off his body.

'I think tonight we'll dispense with the separate sleeping arrangements.'

'What?' Julia started to turn round and then stopped as she realised that turning round would bring her body to body with him.

'This really is a wonderful view,' she blurted out in panic.

'Wonderful,' Silas agreed kindly.

He had put his arm around her—both arms, in fact, Julia discovered.

'I don't think this is a very good idea,' she warned him in a wobbly voice.

'No? Are you sure?'

His mouth was brushing hers. How could such a cool and remote man have such a warm and sensual mouth? Like fire under ice, or her favourite dessert, hot sauce on cold ice cream. Mmm, delicious... Just like the feel of Silas's mouth on her own, in fact. Mmm.

As she sighed her appreciation of his kiss, she moved closer to him and put her own arms around his neck.

His tongue probed her lips, slowly but oh, so deliberately, letting her know that he would not stop until she had given him what he wanted. Her body shivered with pleasure as she let him thrust firmly between her half-parted lips. Oh, but he was good. Or was it just that it was just so long since she had last been kissed? Her whole body had become the ice cream now, melting in the heat of the deliberately slow and sensually symbolic thrust of his tongue within the eager wetness of her mouth.

His hand claimed her breast, moulding it firmly and then caressing it rhythmically, his fingertips teasing her nipple before his hand

slid back so that this palm was rubbing erotically against it, the caress repeated so firmly
and insistently that her whole body began
pulse to the rhythmic movement of his hand.
Instinctively she wanted to return the intimacy
of his touch, to hold the stiff hot flesh of his
erection in her hand so that she could explore
its veined hardness and see his pleasure whilst
she did so.

It had been so long since she had last had
sex. She had truly believed that she wasn't
bothered, but now she realised that she must
be, because she was already aching with fran-
tic need for Silas.

Silas!

Abruptly she broke the kiss.

'What's wrong?'

'We shouldn't be doing this…'

'Of course we should,' Silas told her
promptly. 'We're engaged.'

When she looked at him, he added softly,
'And, more importantly, you want to.'

'Do *you*?'

The way he looked at her as he took hold
of her hand and placed it against his erection
made her heart turn over inside her chest.

'What do you think?' he demanded.

Julia was too caught up in the discovery that his bank account wasn't the only thing about him that was larger than average to make any kind of response.

A part of her was thinking that this couldn't be her, actually thinking of having sex with Silas, but another and much more assertive part was saying it would hate her for ever if she didn't allow it to satisfy the fiercely urgent need that had taken hold of her.

Even so…she had her responsibilities…

'I ought to go over to the hotel and just check…'

'How do I know that isn't just an excuse to sneak off and indulge your shoe habit?' Silas teased her.

She had a shoe habit? She didn't remember. In fact she couldn't think of anything other than what it was going to feel like to lie naked under Silas whilst he filled her with his gorgeous thick strength until he had satisfied the ache that was pulsing from her clitoris right up to her womb.

'Okay, come on,' Silas announced, his voice suddenly crisp. 'Let's get unpacked, and then go down and get some dinner.'

Unpacked? Dinner? There was only one hunger she wanted to satisfy right now. And as for clothes…

Silas watched her with a small satisfied smile. She wanted him and she wanted him badly. That was good. Establishing a sexual bond with her prior to persuading her to marry him might not have been part of his original game plan—sexual satisfaction within their marriage hadn't been particularly high on his original list of priorities—but a plan could be adapted. Why shouldn't he make use of such an excellent opportunity, especially when doing so would be very pleasurable for them both? And not just pleasurable in the short term, but potentially very pleasurable in the long term as well, bonding Julia to him in a way that could only be beneficial to their marriage.

The truth, if he was honest with himself, was that the speed and intensity of his arousal had caught him totally off guard. He prided himself on his sexual self-control, but right now he could feel himself straining and pulsing with his need to push slowly and deeply into Julia's wet heat until she had taken all of him, and then, equally slowly, to ease himself out again before thrusting slickly back in, slowly and deeply, until she raked his back with her nails and held him in her, whilst she moaned her pleasure and urged him to move harder and faster…

Abruptly he made himself think of something else. He might have decided to marry Julia eight years ago, but since he hadn't spent those years fantasising about having sex with her, he saw no reason why he should allow himself to do so now.

He was suddenly and uncomfortably aware that if he hadn't already been planning to marry Julia, then the intensity of his physical desire for her might have been a problem. And there was no place for problems in Silas's life—just as there was no place for situations he could not control.

His mother was a shrewd and emotionally strong woman, but as a young widow she had bowed to the pressure put on her by her late husband's financial advisers and accepted the Foundation's trustees' insistence on helping her to shape and direct the way in which Silas was groomed to take on the role which would one day be his almost from the day of his birth.

The burden of being responsible for the future of the Foundation and its billions of dollars was not one that could be taken on lightly. Her husband, Silas's father, had died before his twenty-fifth birthday, and these trustees even then had already been in their late middle age, considering the heat and excitement of youthful passion something to be deplored and strictly controlled. Through their guidance and teaching Silas had not just learned how to protect the Foundation, but had also absorbed almost from his cradle certain old-fashioned attitudes to life. Silas had, in short, been raised to put the Foundation first, to exercise self-control, and to be practical and unemotional. The trustees were all dead now, but he knew how much they would have approved of his decision to make Julia his wife. He saw what he had learned from the old men who had been his male role models as an asset, and indeed it was one he fully intended to pass on to his own sons.

Julia watched him, wondering what he was thinking and if he was as astonished and bemused by what was happening to them as she was herself.

That was the trouble with Silas: one could never tell what he was thinking.

She picked up her bag and searched for her mobile. She hadn't had time to charge it before leaving Majorca, so she had switched it off to preserve what was left of the battery.

Her fingers closed over her phone and she extracted it from the bottom of her handbag and switched it on, making a small moue as she saw how many messages she had to check through.

'You should upgrade to a BlackBerry,' Silas told her as he observed what she was doing.

'I should. But right now the business isn't making enough money for that.'

Silas frowned. 'I saw Blayne using one.'

'Oh, yes, Nick's got one. But then he does a lot more travelling than anyone else.'

She started to check though her messages, slightly alarmed to see how many there were from her client.

As she played them her alarm became anxiety, and then dismayed disbelief. Switching off her mobile, she turned to Silas.

'I've got to get over to the venue. There's been some kind of mix-up and I need to get it sorted out asap.'

'What kind of mix-up?' Silas demanded.

'When the client asked to look over the private dining room the hotel told her that the booking for the celebratory dinner party had been cancelled. Of course she immediately got in touch with Lucy, and both she and Lucy have been trying to get hold of me to find out what's going on. I've got to get over there. There's obviously been some mistake. I made the booking myself, and there's no way I would have cancelled it—not after all the trouble we had persuading the hotel to let us have exclusive use of the room and the terrace.'

'Can't you phone them?' Silas asked.

Julia shook her head.

'I could, but I'd much rather go over and sort things out in person.'

'I'll come with you,' Silas told her.

'Thank you, but no.' Julia refused his offer firmly. 'This is my problem, not yours. There's obviously been some kind of mix-up, and hopefully it won't take too long to get it sorted out.' She was still wearing the clothes in which she had travelled, and she felt grubby and tired, but her own comfort would have to wait.

Half an hour later, having decided it would be simpler and quicker to walk to the hotel venue, Julia was standing at the reception desk trying to sound calm and professional as she explained who she was and asked to see the hotel manager. Her hope was that she would be able to sort out whatever the problem was prior to announcing her presence to the clients.

However, when she saw the dubious look the immaculately groomed receptionist was giving her, she couldn't help wondering whether it might have been wiser to have taken the time to shower and change, instead of panicking and rushing over here. But of course it was too late to worry about that now.

She was kept waiting in the hotel's reception area for well over fifteen minutes before the hotel manager finally emerged from his office to beckon impassively to her to come forward.

There was no way she intended to discuss the situation in such a public arena, with the reception desk between them and her very much the supplicant on the wrong side of it. So, as diplomatically as she could, Julia curved her mouth into what she hoped was an appealing smile and asked softly if they might talk somewhere more private.

For several perilous seconds she thought that he was going to refuse, but eventually he pursed his lips and said brusquely, 'Very well, then. Come this way.'

The office to which he showed her was much the same as its counterparts all over the world. A large desk dominated the small space, and the chair he waved her into was slightly uncomfortable and too low, whilst his own gave him some extra inches of height he did not in reality possess.

Prêt a Party secured its business by word of mouth, and no matter how frankly she might express her opinions in her personal life, in her professional life Julia had taught herself to speak with a honeyed careful tongue and to use tact and diplomacy at all times. Especially these kinds of times.

As soon as she was seated she smiled and offered a calm apology for the inconvenience being caused by what was obviously a mix-up of some kind before insisting firmly, 'Obviously there has been a clerical error somewhere, because I can assure you that I have not cancelled our booking. You will remember, I know, our negotiations when the original booking was made—'

'Indeed I do. And I also remember it was agreed that you would pay a holding deposit of one half of the estimated bill for the evening.'

'Of course. And I explained your requirement to our clients, who agreed to your terms.'

The manager's mouth thinned ominously.

'But you did not abide by those terms, did you?'

Julia frowned, but managed to stay calm.

'I'm sorry. I don't understand. What do you mean?'

'I mean that you did not forward the sum agreed to us, and, what is more, you ignored the several e-mails I sent to you requesting it—including my final e-mail warning that if payment was not immediately forthcoming the booking would be cancelled.'

'No—there must be some mistake,' Julia protested.

'I have copies of the e-mails here—and I have shown them to your clients.'

Julia couldn't understand what had happened. She could clearly remember receiving the Silverwoods' cheque and passing it over to Nick, who dealt with the accounting side of the business. After receiving the Silverwoods' cheque Nick should have paid it into their bank account and then issued a cheque to the hotel: that was the way in which they worked. Right now, though, what was more important than discovering who had been at fault was ensuring that her clients' event ran smoothly, and as they had arranged.

She would have to throw herself on the hotel manager's mercy—even if right now he looked far from showing her any.

'I can only apologise again,' she tried softly. 'Obviously there has been some mistake...'

'There has been no mistake here,' the manager told her coldly. 'We have e-mailed your accounts department on several occasions, requesting payment of this deposit, and yet we have not once received a reply.'

Small cold fingers of despair gripped Julia's stomach. 'There has obviously been a communication breakdown at our end,' she told the manager, as calmly as she could. 'And of course I apologise for that. As soon as I return to London I shall look into it to find out exactly what has happened. But in the meantime I know that both of us will want to do everything we can to ensure that Mr. and Mrs. Silverwood's celebration is everything that they want it to be.'

The hotel manager gave a dismissive shrug.

'As to that, I have already told them that it is impossible for us to allow them to have exclusive use of the dining room now. And, even if it was, we have not made the necessary arrangements in the kitchen. We cannot simply provide a meal such as they had requested at such short notice.'

Julia was beginning to feel slightly sick. The origination of this event and its smooth running was her responsibility and hers alone. The Silverwoods had come to them on the recommendation of a friend, and right from the start Mrs. Silverwood had made it plain exactly what she wanted and how important the event was. To have to tell her now, at this late stage, that not only could they not have the dining room but also that it was not possible to organise the meal she had planned in such minute detail would not just damage Prêt a Party's reputation—more importantly, it would ruin what should have been a very special event.

Julia did her utmost to put across to the manager all of this, and to appeal to him to think not so much of her error but instead of the unhappiness it would cause their mutual clients if the dinner could not go ahead.

'The hotel is full, and we have many people here who have already booked tables in our dining room. It is, after all, one of the most famous assets of our hotel. Everyone who comes here wants to dine in it and look out over Positano.'

'*Signor*, please.'

'No. I am sorry, but it is just not possible.'

The hotel manager wasn't just standing up now, he was also moving purposefully towards the door, obviously intent on getting rid of her. However, before he reached it it suddenly opened inwards, and a very upset and determined Mrs. Silverwood was pushing her way past the receptionist who had tried to stop her from entering the office.

'Julia, what on earth is going on?' she demanded immediately. 'You assured me that the dining room was booked for our exclusive use, but Signor Bartoli insists that it isn't.'

Silas looked at his watch. He had showered, redressed, dealt with his e-mails and right now he was more than ready for his dinner. Julia had been gone for over an hour—more than enough time in which to sort out a minor misunderstanding.

It took him fifteen minutes to walk to the hotel venue, and precisely fifteen seconds to persuade the harassed-looking receptionist to admit him to her manager's office.

Silas could hear the raised voices even before she opened the door—chief amongst them the hotel manager's.

Julia was standing in a corner of the room looking trapped and white-faced as he harangued her, whilst another woman, whom Silas assumed must be Julia's client, sat sobbing on a chair, demanding to know why her party had been ruined.

'Signor Bartoli?'

As all three occupants of the room turned towards him Silas looked first at Julia. She looked shocked and very worried, her eyes widening as she saw him.

The hotel manager looked as though he were about to burst a blood vessel, his face red with angry frustration, whilst Julia's client looked as any woman would having discovered that a year's worth of careful planning was in ruins.

'Who are you and what do you want?' the enraged manager demanded. 'If you are yet another person here to insist that I throw my guests out of their own dining room in order to accommodate a party that has not been paid for, then—'

'I am the Honourable Julia's fiancé,' Silas answered him calmly, shamelessly making use of Julia's title. 'Perhaps we might talk with one another man to man, *signor*? You are a businessman, but I am sure that you are also a very reasonable and compassionate man,' he added, taking advantage of the momentary silence he had created to remove his chequebook from his pocket.

'I am also sure that it is possible for us to reach a mutually acceptable solution to this present *impasse*. Mr. and Mrs. Silverwood have only the very happiest memories of your hotel, *signor*, and I am sure we would both want them to continue to feel that way. Mrs. Silverwood has set her heart on celebrating here. I am sure that it is not beyond your power to grant her this very special desire, despite the misunderstanding that has occurred. Naturally,

I am prepared to make full recompense to you for the inconvenience this misunderstanding has cost you. Furthermore, I am sure that a man such as yourself has the skills to explain the situation to those guests who are not taking part in the celebrations, and I am equally sure that they will very generously agree to eat their dinner somewhere else in order to accommodate Mr. and Mrs. Silverwood. In fact, I have already spoken to the manager of my own hotel, the Arcadia, on this very subject, and he has confirmed that your guests may dine there—at my expense.'

Without turning his head to look at Julia, Silas told her, 'Perhaps Mrs. Silverwood would like to a have a restorative glass of champagne, Julia, whilst Signor Bartoli and I discuss this matter further.'

It was ten o'clock, and Silas had warned Julia that if she took longer than ten minutes to shower and change then he was going down to dinner without her.

She had managed it in eight minutes flat, and now they were seated opposite one another at a table in the restaurant, having just ordered their food.

'You can't believe I did what?'

'You know what I mean! Paying Signor Bartoli an extra twenty thousand euros on top of the bill to change his mind and let Mr. and Mrs. Silverwood have the dining room after all.' She gave a small disbelieving shake of her head.

'What went wrong?' Silas asked her.

'I don't know,' Julia admitted. 'Our system is that our clients pay all the bills we incur on their behalf themselves, via us. That way we keep our own overheads down and they get to see exactly what the costs are. All we charge them for is our professional services as organisers.'

'Surely when you received those e-mails it must have alerted you to a potential problem.'

'Well, yes, it would have done if I had seen them, but I didn't—' She broke off to smile at the waiter as he brought their first course.

Her stomach was still churning with anxiety-induced adrenalin. The scene in the hotel manager's office had left her feeling so physically and emotionally on edge that the last thing she wanted to do was eat. She didn't want to tell Silas that, though.

It was bad enough that he had witnessed her humiliation and been obliged to rescue her from it, without letting him see how stupidly upset and shaken she still felt.

Silas had scant tolerance of other people's emotional vulnerability, and that was an aspect of his personality that had always made her feel defensive and wary. He always seemed so invulnerable, which highlighted her awareness of her own weaknesses. He seemed to think that in paying the hotel manager to change his mind he had solved the whole problem, but Julia was now sick with worry about how on earth she was going to repay him. The business certainly could not do so. Lucy had confided worriedly to her that they were barely breaking even, never mind making any profit. Julia had no money of her own, and whilst her stepfather was a relatively wealthy man Julia could not imagine asking him to give her twenty thousand euros.

Silas watched her pushing her soup round and not drinking it for several seconds before demanding, 'What's wrong?'

'Nothing. I'm just not hungry.'

'It's over twelve hours since you last ate. How can you not be hungry?'

'I'm just not. But I am tired. In fact, if you don't mind, I think I'll go up to…to bed.'

Silas gave a small shrug.

'If that's what you want to do, go ahead.'

It was his dinner he wanted, not her company, he assured himself, as Julia pushed back her chair and stood up. And that sharp little knife-twist he could feel, of something that was almost pain, wasn't a pain at all. It was just a pang of irritation caused by Julia being Julia.

Julia stared at the figures she had written down on the piece of paper in front of her. Her head was beginning to ache and she felt sick. No matter how much she juggled with the figures, there was just no way she was going to be able to find twenty thousand euros. She didn't like to go into debt and didn't even possess a credit card—but nor did she in the way of savings, either (she bought too many shoes!). Her family was wealthy but their money was all tied up in property—such as the Estate at Amberley and the London flat where she lived—assets that were supposed to be preserved for future Earls and so weren't hers to sell. Perhaps she would have to try and raise a loan—but it was not as if she had any property to borrow against.

Silas picked up his wine glass and looked sombrely at the contents. It held a robust, energetic rioja, with a good parentage, that should have tasted warm and well rounded instead of slightly sour. Or was it his mood that had turned sour and not the wine? Why should that be? Not, surely, because Julia had left him to eat alone? Silas often ate alone. In fact he preferred to. He glanced down at his plate. His steak was cooked just as he liked, but he might just as well have been eating sawdust, he realised, as he pushed his plate away from himself and signalled for the waiter.

As the hotel lift took him up to the suite, he wondered what the hell was happening to him? Why hadn't he simply stayed where he was and finished his meal? Why had both it and the evening lost their flavour and become flat and unappealing without Julia's presence?

Engrossed in the figures in front of her, Julia did not hear the outer door open, or see Silas walk in until he was virtually standing in front of her.

'What's this?' he demanded, picking up the piece of paper and studying it.

'Nothing,' Julia fibbed, but Silas wasn't listening to her. He stared at the small, worried little sums, written down over and over again, and something inside him that he hadn't known was there moved a painful little notch, like the cranking of some long-unused mechanism, its movement all the more agonising because of that.

'You don't seriously think that I expect *you* to repay me, do you?' he demanded sharply.

'Why not? Someone has to,' Julia told him. 'And I know that Lucy can't. The business is barely breaking even, and if the business can't repay you, then naturally I feel morally obliged to do so myself. Because I dealt with the Silverwoods' event.'

Her eyes widened as Silas suddenly screwed up the piece of paper with an almost violent movement of his hand and threw it into the wastepaper bin.

He had no real idea quite why Julia's comment should affect him so strongly, nor why he should feel so enraged because she didn't realise that he didn't want to be repaid.

'You're my fiancée, remember? The money I gave to the hotel manager I gave because I did not wish to see my fiancée being harassed and distressed. Therefore it was for *my* benefit as much as anyone else's. There is no reason for Lucy to know about it and even less for her to pay me back,' he told her grimly.

'But our engagement isn't real,' Julia pointed out. 'And even if it were I'd still want to repay you.'

Silas looked at her. 'Why?'

'Because I would. Because I don't like what it does to a relationship when one person uses the other—financially or in any kind of way. How could you respect me? How could I respect myself if I let you carry me financially? I can't match you for money, Silas, but if we were really a couple I would want to match you in respect and…and…all sorts of other ways…'

Silently Silas digested what she was saying. She had surprised him he admitted. How could this young woman who had admitted openly to a constant need to buy shoes also manifest such a deeply ingrained sense of responsibility and pride? And how could he not have known that she did?

'Since your clients insist they sent you a cheque, and moreover the cheque has been cashed, it seems to me there must have been some kind of accounting mistake. The money must be in Prêt a Party's accounts somewhere. Who deals with the day-to-day finances of the business?'

Julia exhaled slowly, and then told him reluctantly, 'Nick.'

'Blayne?' Silas demanded sharply.

Julia looked away, reluctant to admit to Silas that she was beginning to remember some odd and very worried comments Carly had made before she had left Prêt a Party to marry Ricardo.

Could it be that Nick was doing something fraudulent with the company's money?

Julia was reluctant to speak openly to Silas about her burgeoning suspicions in case she was wrong. Nick might have threatened to punish her for refusing his sexual advances, but there was no way he could have carried out that threat by allowing the booking to be cancelled. The timing simply wasn't right. Unless he had somehow or other tampered with her e-mails…But that would mean that Nick was stealing from his own wife, and why on earth would he do that?

And then she remembered that Nick had wanted to come to Positano with her.

'Now what's wrong?' Silas queried, as he watched the way her expression changed and anxiety shadowed her eyes.

'I was just thinking about Nick,' Julia said.

CHAPTER SIX

JUST thinking about Nick? Hardly. No, what she really meant was that she wanted Blayne, despite having insisted previously that she didn't. And despite, too, having responded physically to *him*.

Silas wasn't used to hearing a woman express desire for another man when she was with him. And he certainly wasn't used to the feelings he was now experiencing. Anger, pain—*jealousy*? What on earth was happening to him?

Oblivious to the interpretation Silas had put on her words, Julia took a deep breath and then asked uncomfortably, 'Silas, you don't think that Nick could be—?'

'I don't think he could be what? So unhappy in his marriage that he should leave Lucy for you?' Silas demanded savagely.

'Leave Lucy for *me*? I've already told you that I don't want him!'

'But you can't stop thinking about him?'

'What? No! I'm not thinking about him like *that*,' Julia protested. 'It's Lucy I'm concerned about.'

When Silas continued to look unconvinced, she told him, 'Nick deals with the financial side of the business, and I can't help wondering...'

It was hard to come out and say what she was actually thinking, but she could see from Silas's expression that she was going to have to—unless she wanted him to continue to think she wanted Nick. Although quite why it suddenly seemed so very important to convince him that she didn't, and that there was no one else in her life, she wasn't prepared to analyse too much.

Instead she took a deep breath and said uncomfortably, 'I'm probably being stupid about this, but I can't help worrying that Nick might be...' This was so difficult! 'Silas, you don't think he could be doing anything wrong, do you?' she appealed anxiously.

'Wrong? What kind of wrong?'

When she began to chew anxiously on her bottom lip and looked uneasy, Silas suddenly realised what she was trying to say.

'You think that Blayne might be defrauding the business?'

Relief replaced Julia's earlier discomfort. 'Yes! Well, no. I don't know. I mean, why should he, when he's married to Lucy? But I *know* that I never saw those e-mails from the hotel. I know that I passed the cheque on to Nick, along with the invoices it was supposed to cover.'

'You said yourself that the business was struggling to make money—maybe the situation is worse than you know and Blayne simply couldn't pay out the deposits because there wasn't enough money?'

'In that case why didn't he say something to me? Warn me? He was very angry that he wasn't going to be coming to Positano with me. I thought it was because I'd told him I wasn't going to have sex with him, but if he knew that there was going to be a problem here… Oh, Silas, I just don't know what to think or do. Lucy is one of my two closest friends. Prêt a Party is her business. The last thing I want is to do something that might hurt her.'

It was only natural that he should be relieved to discover that Julia had not lied to him, Silas assured himself. But a taunting inner voice told him mockingly, Relieved, yes. But surely not almost euphoric?

'Would you like me to make some discreet enquiries?'

'I don't know,' Julia admitted. 'Maybe if you left it until I've been able to speak to Lucy and…and check everything.'

'You're worried that Lucy might be implicated as well?' Silas guessed.

'No! Lucy would never do anything dishonest.'

'But you think that Blayne could have involved her in something *he* has done that is dishonest?'

'I don't know, Silas…and, like I just said, I don't want to do anything that could hurt her. I feel so sorry for her, and I feel a bit guilty as well. If it hadn't been for me she would never have met Nick in the first place.'

'You can't say that. She might still have met him without you.'

She looked so distressed that Silas immediately found he wanted to comfort her. And not just verbally, he realised, and he discovered that somehow or other he had moved closer to her.

'I am grateful to you for what you did at the hotel, Silas,' Julia told him huskily. Silas was being so very kind and understanding.

'I just wish...' She stopped speaking as Silas reached out and drew her purposefully into his arms.

'Why don't we forget about Prêt a Party and focus on this instead?'

So much had happened that she had almost forgotten the thrill of anticipation and excitement she had felt earlier. Almost, but not entirely. And now immediately it was back, her pleasure even hotter and sweeter this time as Silas kissed her with deliberate thoroughness.

'Mmm.' Julia slipped her arms round his neck to hold him closer as she savoured the deepening passion of his kiss, and then shivered in voluptuous pleasure as his hands sculpted the curves of her body before taking possession of her breasts.

Her own arousal was hot and fiery and immediate. Behind her closed eyelids she could see erotic images of them together—Silas's hands and mouth on her naked body, possessing it and her. She could see herself writhing in eager urgency whilst his lips played erotically with the tight, hot jut of her nipples, his hand slipping between her legs to open her to his sensual exploration.

But who needed to imagine when what he was already doing to her was so effective? She loved the way his fingertips stroked her breast, so slowly and tantalisingly, and then drew erotically on her waiting nipple, savouring its hardness through the layers of fabric.

He lifted his mouth from hers and started to kiss her jaw, causing her to arch back her head so that he could plunder the soft, sweet flesh of her throat, and then move lower to that special secret place where her neck ran into her shoulder and where just the warmth of his breath was enough to make her shudder in wanton need.

Being held, and touched and kissed like this, with nothing to do other than let Silas build her arousal, was the most deliciously sensual and self-indulgent pleasure. She exhaled slowly on a luxuriant sigh of delight and stroked her fingertips through the thick hair at the back of his neck. His flesh felt warm and firm, and oh, so wonderfully male. A feeling of harmony and happiness, of *rightfulness*, stroked slowly through her like a delicious extra layer of physical pleasure. She traced the curve of his neck and then the rigid hardness of his collarbone with delicate fingertips, savouring his male difference.

'Mmm. Lovely strong muscles.'

The approving, almost purring pleasure in her voice caused Silas to tug urgently on her nipple and then bite gently at her earlobe before whispering thickly, 'Why don't we get rid of some of these clothes?'

Beneath his hands her body arched fiercely in eager response.

'I thought you were never going to ask,' Julia admitted huskily.

Silas had switched off the electric lights, but the doors to the balcony were open and uncurtained. The sky was so bright with stars and a full moon that more than enough silver light was shining down on them for him to see her clearly. Her eyes shone with liquid desire, her lips slightly swollen and flushed with colour from his kisses. Not even the fact that she was fully dressed could conceal her arousal: the stiff thrust of her nipples was plainly visible. He reached out and traced a slow circle with his fingertip around the one he had been caressing, watching with totally male satisfaction as her whole body tightened and she exhaled fiercely. Inside his head he could already see the naked flesh of her breast, creamy pale against the puckered darkness of her nipple; he could feel the way her body would shudder as he teased the tight peak with the tip of his tongue before taking it fully into his mouth. He could even hear her wild cry of erotic pleasure as she called out to him to satisfy her.

What was Silas waiting for? Julia looked up at him questioningly, and then reached out to touch the hard ridge of his erection, stroking its fabric-covered heat with delicate fingertips, seeking and finding the sensitive place where its head bulged thickly from his foreskin.

Silas discovered that he could scarcely bear to so much as breathe as he stood stiff and still whilst her fingertip mapped and teased him, in case somehow he missed a fraction of the almost unbearable pleasure of her touch.

It wasn't very often that Silas felt any need to give thanks for the gifts life had given him—he was, after all, a man who dealt in practicalities, not emotions—but suddenly he recognised that unexpectedly he had received a very special life-enhancing bonus. He wanted Julia and she wanted him, and the desire between them was so hot and so fierce, so immediate and so damned right, that it almost made their marriage a necessity in its own right.

Whatever he had envisaged when he had thought about marriage to Julia, it had not been that he would feel like this. But now that he did feel like this... Silas gave a low, tormented moan of raw male pleasure as her fingertips slowly and rhythmically worked his foreskin over the pulsing head of his penis, whilst she used her free hand to unzip his trousers and then unfasten his belt.

She wanted them to get naked? Well, so did he.

Silas could be both ruthless and inventive when he wanted to be, Julia decided happily only seconds later, as her clothes were removed so speedily and determinedly that it seemed to her that one minute she was fully dressed and the next she was standing in the moonlight wearing only her very brief lace thong, with Silas kneeling on the floor in front of her. Or rather she was almost wearing it. Because Silas had slid his hands beneath the thin lace-covered elastic that had been resting on her hips and was circling her belly button with his tongue-tip.

His hands moved to her bottom, kneading the rounded flesh whilst his tongue teased a line of fire just above the triangle of lace fabric covering the firm, mound of her pubic bone.

He had loved one hand from her bottom and was sliding it between her legs, stroking the sensitive flesh on the inside of her thighs, his touch making her sigh with soft pleasure.

Somehow the warmth of his lips teasing the sensual spot just above the soft dark curls that covered her mound, the slow, explorative stroke of his fingers as they moved up her thigh and under the lacy barrier between them, and the eager swelling of the soft fleshy lips concealing her sex seemed to link the two parts of her body together via an almost electric invisible arc of sizzlingly erotic pleasure. It made her want to push deeper into his touch. It made her want to wantonly demand that he give her more, so very much more. It made her want to urge him to make those tiny flutters of sensation she could feel pulsing deep inside her wet heat become much stronger and fiercer. In short, it made her want…

'Oh, Silas…' she groaned warningly, her helpless moan of pleasure turning to a sharp gasp as his fingertip stroked through her wetness to caress her clitoris. Almost immediately her body was seized with a violent shudder of delight that left her quivering helplessly whilst Silas picked her up and carried her over to the bed, placing her on it and then stripping off his clothes whilst she lay watching him.

In all the years they had known one another she had never so much as seen him wearing a pair of swimming shorts, she realised as her eager gaze delighted in the sight of his wide shoulders tapering down to a flat stomach. His skin was lightly tanned, his body hair dark and soft-looking, lightly covering his chest but making an erotically denser line down the centre of his body before thickening out around his penis.

'Mmm...' Julia purred happily as she reached up to touch him. 'You've got a gorgeous, sexy body, Silas. Just looking at it makes me melt inside with anticipation.'

He had always known that she had a tendency to be outspoken and say whatever came into her head, but he hadn't known just how much pleasure that outspokenness was going to give him, Silas thought, as a certain part of his 'gorgeous, sexy body' showed its appreciation of her compliment by stiffening even more.

'Mmm.' Julia reached out and ran one fingertip around the engorged glossy head, her touch making Silas fight to smother a groan of pleasure and a small bead of milky fluid began to form.

Very gently Julia caught it with her fingertip and looked up at Silas, laughing softly. 'Ooh. Baby gravy.'

'You want my baby?' Silas heard himself demanding thickly.

'Silas…' Julia began to protest. But Silas was already kissing her so passionately that it was impossible for her to say or do anything other than respond to him.

'I'd forgotten just how good skin on skin feels,' Julia murmured sleepily as she snuggled into Silas, her hand spread flat against his chest, registering the post-orgasm slowing of his heartbeat.

'Has it been a long time since the last time, then?' Silas asked her casually.

'Aeons,' Julia admitted frankly. 'In fact so long that I can hardly remember it. You know what it's like, Silas. When you're in your teens and you've got all those hormones jumping about all over the place sex is all you can think about, but then somehow life takes over, doesn't it? Setting up the business and then running it has taken up so much time there just hasn't been any left for anything else. Even if

I had met someone I wanted to go to bed with, I wouldn't have had time.'

'You met Blayne,' Silas reminded her.

'Well, yes, but Nick dropped me for Lucy before we'd got as far as having sex.'

'So your passionate response is more likely to be the result of frustration than any actual desire for me?' Silas probed.

'Who said I was frustrated?' Julia demanded.

'You did.'

'No, I didn't. I said I'd forgotten how good skin on skin felt. And that's different. After all, I've got Roger to make sure I don't get frustrated.'

'Roger?' Silas queried.

'Yes Roger. My Rabbit. My *vibrator*,' Julia explained, when he looked at her uncomprehendingly, a smile dimpling the corners of her mouth. 'Jessica Rabbit—a single girl's best friend. Only I call mine Roger because he...'

Silas started to laugh. 'Okay, yes—I get it, Roger as in ''to roger''—the good old-fashioned English word.'

'A vibrator's okay, but no way can it compare with being with you. It was really good for me, Silas,' Julia told him softly. 'In fact...' She hesitated, her fingers curling into the soft hair on his chest, her lashes sweeping down to conceal her expression, but Silas could still see the heat warming her face.

'In fact?' he encouraged, noting in fascinated male bewilderment that *now* she was blushing.

The dark lashes lifted and she was looking at him with those huge amazing eyes of hers.

'In fact, it was the best sex I have ever had,' she admitted huskily.

A sensation that was both physical and emotional, and so strong that momentarily it almost stopped his heartbeat, gripped Silas by the throat. It had to be caused by the realisation that he was being given the perfect opportunity to achieve his goal, he told himself practically, before saying, 'Really? Good enough to make it worthwhile turning this fake engagement of ours into a real marriage?'

'What? You're joking!'

Silas shook his head. 'No. I'm completely serious,' he told her truthfully.

'But…but why on earth would you want to marry me?' Julia demanded, her forehead pleating into a small frown.

'Oh, the usual reasons,' Silas told her lightly. 'You turn me on. You give good head. And I love the way you yell, "Siii—lasss!" when you come.'

Julia giggled and punched him playfully on his arm.

'Those are not good reasons.'

'I can't think of any better,' Silas told her. 'Unless it's the pleasure I get from filling you with baby gravy.'

Julia laughed, and then stopped, her face anxious.

'Silas, you don't think…?'

'I don't think what?'

Julia started to chew her bottom lip.

'We didn't use a condom, and I'm not using any contraception. What are we going to do?'

'You want kids, don't you?'

'Yes, of course.' And that speaking of them as 'we' had turned her heart to melting choc-olate, Julia realised.

'So, what are we waiting for?'

'Silas!' Julia protested as he turned to reach for her.

'Okay, maybe it would not be such a good idea for you to walk down the aisle wearing a tent. We'd better buy some condoms—and bring the wedding forward.'

Quite how it was possible over the course of two short days for her to go from thinking of Silas as someone she preferred to see as little of as possible to knowing that she was passionately in love with him and wanted to spend the rest of her life with him, preferably making babies, Julia was far too blissed-out and far too sexed-out to worry about.

All she needed to make her whole world perfect was Silas. Silas and a bed. Silas and a shower large enough for two people. Silas and a magical walk along the seashore, with shadows deep enough for them to hide in body to body whilst their shared passion drove them to forget everything but one another. Silas, whose taste she still had on her tongue and whose scent she could still smell on her skin and in her hair. Silas, who always gave that funny little grunt before he gave in to his own orgasm. Silas who filled her and thrilled her, who satisfied her and aroused her, as no other man ever had done or would do.

She was obsessed with him, Julia admitted cheerfully to herself, her mouth curving into a wide, happy smile. Obsessed with him and totally, totally besotted by him. She felt like a particularly smug Bridget Jones-type singleton. The kind who would write deliriously in her diary, *2 days and 20-plus shags*. Silas had to be the world's best lover, even if he protested generously that her partisan enthusiasm was encouraging him to previously unreached heights.

Only this morning he had cupped her face and kissed her nose as the sweat of passion dried on their damp bodies, and told her softly, 'Don't ever take off those rose-coloured glasses you view me through, will you.'

Rose-coloured glasses? As if! The wonderful thing about falling in love with Silas was that she already knew everything there was to know about him, so there couldn't be any unpleasant shocks waiting to wreck their relationship.

'Julia, my dear, have I told you how wonderful all of this is?' Mrs. Silverwood enthused emotionally as she left her guests to come and stand with Julia. 'And all thanks to your wonderful fiancé. I do not know what we would have done if he hadn't managed to persuade the hotel manager to relent.'

On the other side of the restaurant Silas, whom the Silverwoods had insisted on including in their dinner party, finished his champagne and enjoyed himself watching Julia. He had laughed more in these last two days than he had laughed in the whole of the rest of his life. Laughed more and loved more too.

He sincerely hoped that their children would inherit their mother's blithe spirits and sense of humour. Their children. Desire hardened his body, causing him to move discreetly back into the shadows. Sex with Julia was like no sex he had ever had before. He simply couldn't get enough of her, and when his body did cry enough he was filled with a sense of such intense satisfaction that he had no past experience in his life he could compare it to.

This sexual hunger for one another that had overtaken them both had brought a whole new urgency to his determination to marry Julia. The end of the year was way too long to wait. He wanted to tie her to him now, as tightly and permanently as he could. Which was why he had spent hours on the telephone this afternoon, whilst she had been checking over the final arrangements for the dinner. The result was worth the time he had spent, though, even if he *had* had to twist the arms of both the American and British Ambassadors just slightly in order to get what he wanted. Now all he had to do was persuade Julia.

It was four o'clock in the morning, and the streets of Positano were empty as Silas and Julia walked arm in arm back to their own hotel.

'The Silverwoods seemed pleased with the way the event went,' Silas commented.

'Yes, thanks to you. I nearly died when the hotel chef threw that tantrum yesterday and threatened to walk out. That was really quick thinking on your part, to let him think that the chef from the Arcadia would be happy to take over.'

Silas laughed. 'Quick thinking, maybe, but not entirely true. Still, it did the trick. Am I right in thinking that now we've got ten days before we need to be in Marbella for Dorland's party?'

'The party isn't for another ten days,' Julia agreed. 'But we'll have to be there well before that in order to make sure everything is properly organised.'

'How well before?' Silas asked. 'Will three days be enough?'

'At a pinch,' Julia agreed. 'Why?'

They had almost reached the hotel and Silas stopped walking, drawing her into the shadows with him as he leaned back against a convenient wall, his hands on her hips, guiding her between his parted legs.

Just the scent of him was enough to turn her on. Julia pressed closer to him and lifted her face for his kiss.

'Let's not wait to get married.'

His voice was thick and raw, sending a shudder of pleasure jolting through her whilst her heart thudded out a stunned tattoo.

'What—what do you mean?' she demanded uncertainly.

'I mean, let's not wait to get married. Let's do it now. Here in Italy.'

His words fell honey-sweet against their ears; her heart lifted in excited pleasure. So far neither of them had spoken the 'L' word, but, knowing him as she did, that he should feel such an urgency to commit to her told her just how he felt about her. Even so...

'Silas, we can't,' she protested.

'Of course we can. I've already checked it out. We could be married within the week— less, if I put some more pressure on our Ambassador.'

'Why the rush?' she teased him. 'Don't you trust me?'

Silas laughed. 'Yes, I trust *you*. But I'm not sure that I trust the condoms to withstand the rigours we've been subjecting them to.'

Julia giggled.

'Silas, we couldn't...could we?' she breathed excitedly.

'You want to?'

She closed her eyes and then opened them again.

'Do I want to be your wife and have guaranteed wonderful sex for the rest of my life? Of course I do,' she told him extravagantly. 'But what about the family...what about Gramps?'

'We could still have a religious blessing in Amberley Church, and even a reaffirmation of our vows and a formal post-wedding breakfast afterwards, if that is what you want.'

'What I want? All I want is you,' Julia told him simply, and she raised herself up on her toes to kiss him.

CHAPTER SEVEN

'I STILL can't believe we're actually doing this,' Julia whispered nervously to Silas as they stood side by side waiting for their papers to be checked. The American Embassy had recommended that they consult an Italian official well versed in the complexities of the correct procedure to enable other nationals to marry in Italy, and, with a speed that had impressed Julia, all the necessary paperwork had been assembled and submitted. And here they were, just an hour or so short of five days after Silas had suggested they do so, actually about to be married to one another.

'It will be a civil ceremony,' Silas had told her.

'Oh, but that will make whatever we do at home all the more special,' Julia had told him in delight. 'It would be really cool if we could reaffirm our vows at Amberley, like you suggested, Silas. Almost like having a second wedding.'

173

Since the Monckford Diamond was still in New York, Julia had no engagement ring to wear with one of the matching plain gold bands she and Silas had chosen in a small jeweller's, down a narrow side street in Rome.

Emotional tears filled Julia's eyes as they stood together and made their vows. In some strange way being alone together actually made exchanging them all the more special.

As she slid Silas's ring onto his finger she bent her head and brushed it with her lips, promising him silently, *I shall love you for ever.*

She had discovered that Silas was not a man who found talking about his emotions easy. But she was sure he loved her, even though he had not said so. He had married her, after all. A small naughty smile curved her mouth. Before they celebrated their first wedding anniversary she would have taught him to say that he loved her, and that was a promise to herself she was not going to break.

They had agreed that they wouldn't wear their rings until they could go back to England and tell her grandfather what they had done.

'I don't want him to hear about it via Ma's cleaning lady and Dorland's wretched magazine,' Julia had told Silas when they had been discussing the matter.

'Fine—that's okay by me,' Silas had agreed.

Her husband. Julia looked up at Silas, her face glowing with happiness. They would have one night together here in Rome before they flew to Spain tomorrow, and Silas had booked them into the most wonderful hotel.

'I thought we'd go straight back to the hotel,' Silas told her now. 'Unless you'd prefer to do something else?'

'What? Rather than go to bed with you? No way,' Julia told him, shaking her head.

It was so refreshing to be with Julia, Silas acknowledged. She never tried to play controlling mind games, and he loved the way she was so open with him about her sexual desire for him. Not that their mutual sexual desire for one another was the only thing they shared. She was passionately committed to seeing Amberley preserved for future generations— but not, as she had put it, '…like some kind of museum. Amberley—the real Amberley, as it is today—is what it is because of the way each generation had lived in it, because it has been a real home. Not because it has been kept exactly as it was when it was first built. I know Gramps opens it to the public for several months a year, and I know that the state rooms are too grand really to live in…'

'So what would you do with them?' Silas had asked.

'Oh, all sorts of things. We could hold musical evenings in the green salon, so that young musicians could play Handel in the kind of setting for which he wrote his music. We could have literary readings in the library. We could do things with the house and for it that would benefit other people as well. Imagine what it would mean to children learning to play an instrument to be able to have some of their lessons in the green salon, for instance. And then there's the home farm. It know it's a bit run down now, but there's more than enough land for us to have rare varieties of free range hens and ducks…'

'My life is focused on New York,' he had reminded her. 'I have a duty and a responsibility toward the Foundation.'

'I know that. But we could travel between Amberley and New York, couldn't we?'

'Of course.'

She had wrinkled her nose at him in that delicious semi-teasing way she had, and then said hesitantly, 'Silas, I'm afraid I don't know very much about the workings of the Foundation. You're going to have to explain to me exactly how it runs and what *if anything* I can do to help you.'

Yes, he had every right to congratulate himself on his perspicacity in deciding to marry Julia, Silas decided. She was, as he had told his mother on Julia's eighteenth birthday, the perfect wife for him.

The hotel Silas had booked them into was old and elegant, hidden away down a maze of narrow streets which opened out into a quiet piazza, where an ornamental fountain splashed water down into an ornately carved marble basin and equally ornate marble statues stood on marble plinths. The austere grandeur of so much marble was broken up by huge classically shaped urns filled with a tumbling mass of flowers.

Their own suite had a balcony that over-
looked the piazza, and Julia glanced up towards it now, a delicious thrill of excitement
gilding her happiness as she anticipated what
lay ahead.

Having sex with Silas was always wonderful, but this time would be extra special—because this time they would be doing it as husband and wife.

She looked down at her ring. She couldn't
wear it permanently yet, of course. If she did
someone was bound to see it.

'I thought we'd have dinner in the suite tonight,' Silas told her as they walked into the
hotel foyer. 'But first there's something I want
to show you.' He took hold of her arm, guiding
her down a dark vaulted corridor, suddenly
stopping to demand, 'Where's your hat?'

'Here,' Julia told him, showing him the hat
she was holding in her other hand. She had
thought that he would laugh, or even object,
when she had insisted on wearing the pretty
semi-formal straw hat for their marriage, but
instead he had actually given a small nod of
approval.

They had reached a set of highly polished heavy wooden doors, which Silas opened for her.

Beyond them lay another corridor, its walls plain, almost roughly hewn stone, and Julia shivered as she felt the cold coming off them, turning to look enquiringly at Silas.

'The hotel has its own private chapel, where the family who owned the original house used to celebrate Mass. It was a condition that the family made when they sold the house that lighted candles would always be kept burning in the chapel, and that it would always be open to those who wanted to come here to pray and to give thanks.'

They had reached another set of huge double doors. A little hesitantly, Julia looked at Silas.

Smiling at her, he reached out and took her hat from her, and set it very gently on her head.

'That is why I have brought you here, Julia. So that I can give thanks, and because I sensed when we were being married that a part of you was thinking of the church at Amberley.'

Silas was opening the doors. Beyond them Julia could see candlelight, blurred by her own emotional tears.

Taking hold of her hand, Silas led her into the chapel, their footsteps echoing on the worn stone floor.

Silently they walked past the empty pews towards the altar, beyond which an ancient stained glass window reflected the light of the candles. The air smelled of age and damp and that indefinable smell of old churches: a mixture of incense and peace and faith, all bound together with humility and acceptance.

Julia bowed her head. Silas was still holding her hand. She watched as he removed both their rings and then handed her his own.

Silently they exchanged rings. Could there be anything more profound or meaningful than this? Julia wondered. Automatically she knelt in prayer, as she had been taught to do as a small child. This might not be her family church, or her religion, but its spirituality reached out to her and touched her like angels' wings. Even Silas was standing with his head bent, as though he too felt the same sense of awe and humility she was experiencing.

'Silas, thank you.'

They had just walked into their suite, and as he locked the door Silas cocked an enquiring eyebrow and demanded, 'What for?'

'For what you just did. The chapel. My hat. Understanding how I felt. Everything.'

'You've got just under an hour to get changed before dinner.'

It was silly of her to feel disappointed, and even more silly of her to feel hurt because Silas was changing the subject—cutting her off, almost, as though her emotional words irritated him. She had felt so close to him in the chapel, but now she was suddenly aware of how he was distancing himself from her.

His mobile started to ring, and he turned away from her to answer it, but not before Julia heard a girlish female voice exclaiming, 'Silas, darling—surprise! It's me—Aimee!'

Automatically Julia stiffened, but Silas was already walking away from her, his voice too low for her to hear what he was saying as he stepped out onto the balcony.

Aimee DeTroite was a high-maintenance New York socialite heiress, whose sexual adventures had been the subject of a great deal of celebrity gossip. Private videos of her having sex with a variety of male partners—consecutively and concurrently—had apparently been stolen from her apartment and then shown over the Internet to whoever was prepared to view them. She had the reputation of being an extremely difficult and very spoiled young woman, who claimed that her famous tantrums were not caused by an over-fondness for the white powder, as some articles had claimed, but instead by the fact that she was 'bi-polar'.

Of course Silas knew other women, and had women friends—had had other lovers, Julia told herself stoutly. The fact that one of them had chosen to telephone him now might be bad timing, but she was hardly to be blamed for that, and neither was Silas. And calling a man 'darling' hardly meant anything at all any more! Everyone did it. Even Silas when he was talking to her—in public.

Outside on the balcony Silas's fingers tightened on his mobile. He had no idea how Aimee had managed to get hold of his new mobile number, but he wasn't going to waste any time asking her.

'Silas, how could you do this to me? How could you get engaged to someone else when you know how much I love you? I won't let her have you—you know that, don't you? You're mine, Silas. Mine!'

Her voice had started to rise in familiar hysteria. As Silas switched off his mobile, cutting her off, he could hear her starting to scream at him. Grimly he looked into the bedroom, wondering if Julia had heard. If she was upset... He started to frown, his earlier unfamiliar mood of lighthearted tenderness flattened by Aimee's unwanted telephone call. Of course it made sense for practical reasons that he didn't want Julia to hear another woman telephoning him on *their* wedding night. But that didn't totally explain the anger he was feeling because Aimee had intruded on his privacy with Julia.

'Is everything all right?' Julia asked as lightly as she could when Silas stepped back inside the room.

'Everything's fine.' Silas's voice was curt, and she could see that he was frowning. 'Why do you ask?'

'No reason.' Julia fibbed.

Her earlier happiness had vanished, and she was miserably aware both of Silas's withdrawal from her and the fact that another woman was responsible for it.

He was handling things very badly, Silas acknowledged as he registered Julia's small intake of breath and the look in her eyes.

'I'd forgotten I'd promised Aimee I'd buy some tickets for a charity benefit she's organising.'

Julia forced herself to smile. 'I know you dated her at one time.' Thanks to Nick, who had made a point of telling her.

'I have *never* dated Aimee,' Silas denied forcefully. 'I simply know her, that's all.'

'But what about that video when you and she—' Julia blurted out.

'That was—' Silas broke off, and tried to control the angry thumping of his heart. Was he going to be forever pursued by Aimee's malice and the lies she had told about him and their supposed relationship? A relationship that was nothing more than a figment of her own fantasies.

'I just don't want to talk about this, Julia. I am married to you, and that should tell you all you need to know about my relationship with you.' Silas's voice was clipped and sharp.

Julia didn't say anything, but it perturbed her that Silas should be so angrily vehement—almost excessively so, in fact. It was so out of character for him. The action of a man with something to hide?

She didn't want to pursue such thoughts, Julia told herself firmly, and she wasn't going to do so.

They had eaten—a delicious meal—and talked, and Julia rather suspected that she had drunk just a little too much champagne. And now every bit of her was fizzing with anticipatory excitement as Silas reached for her hand and drew her towards him.

The phone call he had received earlier and the woman who had made it had been firmly and determinedly banished from her thoughts. This was, after all, her wedding night, *their* wedding night, and no way was she going to let another woman spoil it.

'I still can't believe that we're married,' she whispered. 'You and me, of all people!'

Silas was cupping her face in his hands and it was impossible for her to say any more, because he was slowly and deliberately kissing her mouth with individual kisses that tasted every curve and angle of her lips. His tongue-tip began to probe deeper, making her moan and cling tightly to him. All she was wearing was a pretty silk chiffon wrap, which she had tied around herself, half uncertain about whether or not she had gone too far in deciding to leave off her underwear.

Now, though, the knowledge that there was so little to come between her flesh and Silas's touch was a potent aphrodisiac that added to her excitement and arousal.

'You are a complete and total sensualist. You know that, don't you?' Silas demanded thickly as he rubbed his palm slowly over her chiffon-covered nipple, enjoying watching the pleasure darken her eyes as much as he was enjoying the feel of her hard nipple, growing tighter between his rhythmically plucking fingers.

Already beyond logical conversation, Julia could only moan and grind her hips eagerly against him. The silk wrap was so sheer that it barely veiled her body, the light shining through it to pick out the dark, sensual ripeness of the aureoles of flesh surrounding her nipples as well as her nipples themselves. It was tied at the front, and when she moved Silas kept getting brief, tormenting glimpses of bare flesh.

He parted the fabric, his hand gripping her naked hip as he bent his head and drew one chiffon-covered nipple into his mouth, caressing it with his tongue-tip whilst Julia writhed helplessly in erotic delight.

But that pleasure was nothing compared to what she felt when Silas caressed the eager wetness of her waiting sex, stroking the full length of her from back to front in a caress that made her cry out and arch into his touch, then cry out again as he played delicately with her clit, nurturing its tight bud into ripe fullness before he finally gave in to her incoherent pleas and slid his fingers into her hot waiting wetness, making her climax so violently that Julia was half afraid she might actually pass out.

'Oh, Silas, that was heavenly.' She wept emotionally as he held her shuddering body. 'Purr-fect. Who would ever have thought that being married to you could be like this?'

'I'm going to take that as a compliment,' Silas told her dryly, as he picked her up and carried her over to the waiting bed.

Laughter gurgled in Julia's throat as she leaned over and kissed him.

'And I'm going to take you as well—unless you've got some objection?'

'No objection. Just a warning that I probably won't come again. Not after an orgasm like that,' Julia cautioned him.

'Want to bet?' Silas asked her.

He was just leaning over her when the telephone started to ring. Immediately Julia stiffened. Was it Aimee ringing him again?

Silas released her and reached for the room telephone at the same moment as she recognised that it was not his mobile ringing.

'That was the reception desk, wanting to know if we'd booked a car. I told them they'd got the wrong room. Now, where were we?' Silas asked softly.

No way was she going to let Aimee spoil what she was enjoying with Silas, Julia assured herself as he took her back in his arms. She closed her eyes tightly, willing herself not to think of anything or anyone other than the two of them and what they were sharing, and gave herself over completely to the physical delight of his hands on her body.

An hour later, after the final ripples of their shared climax had died away and Silas had gathered her into his arms to draw her close to him, Julia decided blissfully that there could be no greater happiness than this, and that she had been silly to worry about that earlier phone call.

She was almost on the verge of falling asleep when she remembered something very important.

'Silas!' she gasped urgently.

'What?'

'We didn't use a condom.'

'No, we didn't, did we?'

If Silas wasn't concerned that they might be risking her conceiving his child, then he couldn't possibly be involved with another woman could he? She had been silly to worry, Julia reassured herself.

CHAPTER EIGHT

MARBELLA in September: the month of summer when the tiresome tourist crowds had gone, along with their noisy children, and the only visitors were those who were rich enough or A-list enough to know that this was the time to be here. Or at least that was what most of the guests invited to Dorland's party were likely to believe, Julia thought cynically, as the chauffeur-driven limo swept them up to the main entrance of Marbella's *luxe de luxe* home from home for the celebrity set—the world famous Alfonso Club, Golf Resort and Spa—or the Alfonso, as most of those in the know referred to the hotel a European prince had created from what had originally been merely a family *finca*, or rural property.

Supposedly, sooner or later everyone who was anyone stayed at the Alfonso. Her smile deepened as she reflected on how very different this fashionable celebrity watering hole was from the hotel they had stayed at in Rome.

Marbella, like St Tropez, St Moritz and a handful of other places worldwide, had held on to its exalted status through many decades. Julia suspected that nowhere else in the world, apart from possibly Palm Springs, was home to quite so many nipped and tucked seventy-something women pretending to be thirty-something. They came here in the summer to bask in the sunshine, like so many stick-thin locusts, bronzing their leathery bodies before retreating to some discreet Swiss clinic to be pampered and prepared for another summer.

Marbella was like nowhere else, being a place where it was almost *de rigueur* to sport a tan, a proper hairdo, diamanté-studded sunglasses and gold leather Gucci-style loafers.

Not that Marbella didn't attract the younger celebrity crowd—it did, and in droves, a fact which Dorland had recognised when he elected to throw his end-of-summer bash here.

Silas had booked them into one of the club's private villas, and as they were shown to it Julia decided she would have to do something about extending her wardrobe. She had seen how sad her small case looked in contrast to the mounds of Louis Vuitton being removed from limousine boots. Already she had spotted at least three famous film stars, plus an all girl-group and their entourage, all of whom she knew had been invited to Dorland's party.

To Julia's delight their villa not only had its own private garden, it also had its own private swimming pool.

'Oh, Silas, this is just too blissful,' she exclaimed happily as she stood looking out of the villa's patio doors towards the pool.

'I thought you'd like it,' Silas agreed, making her both laugh and blush at the same time.

'Just because I happened to say that I'd love to swim naked with you and then have sex outside, in the open air, that doesn't mean you had to find a way to make it possible,' she told him.

'Meaning that now that I have, you've changed your mind?'

'No way,' Julia assured him vehemently. 'Though I'll have to go and find Dorland later.' She gave a small shudder. 'I don't want any more traumas or mistakes of the kind we had in Positano. I still can't believe that actually happened. What is it?' she demanded, when she saw the way Silas was looking at her.

'I've had an e-mail from the person I asked to make some discreet enquiries into both Blayne and Prêt a Party.'

'And?'

'Let's get settled in first. You must be hungry. I'll order something from Room Service, shall I?'

'Silas, it's bad, isn't it?' Julia guessed.

'Let's get sorted out first.'

Julia reached out and touched his arm, sensing that he was trying to distract her.

'No, please tell me now.' She could see from his face that Silas was beginning to wish he hadn't said anything. 'I know you only want to protect me, but I'm not a little girl any more,' she told him gently. 'And Lucy is my friend.'

'All right. But at least let's sit down.'

Her mouth had gone dry, Julia realised as Silas sat in one of the comfortable easy chairs and she perched on the arm of it next to him.

'From what my source has discovered—and I've no reason to doubt him; I've used him in the past to investigate sensitive issues for me— it looks very much as though Prêt a Party has some very serious financial problems.'

'Oh, Silas.' Julia placed her fingertips to her mouth, her eyes shadowing with distress.

'There's worse, I'm afraid. It seems that there is every likelihood that Blayne has been defrauding the business—and Lucy herself as well.'

'Oh, no! Poor Lucy—but how can that have happened? Lucy is always complaining that her trustee won't let her touch her trust fund without his say-so.'

'Maybe not, but he has allowed her to guarantee Prêt a Party's overdraft facilities. And that means that the bank has been able to call upon her to clear it via her trust fund. From what my source has discovered, it seems that large amounts of money have been withdrawn from the business by Blayne, which have caused an overdraft that Lucy has had to make good. It seems that there is no real business reason why he should have withdrawn such large amounts, and my source suspects they have gone straight into his own pocket—if Lucy isn't aware of what he's doing.'

'She can't be.' Julia defended her friend immediately. 'Lucy is scrupulously honest, Silas.'

'Maybe she was. But she loves Blayne, and if he has been pressuring her...'

'No.' Julia shook her head vigorously. 'No matter how much Lucy loves Nick, she would never agree to anything underhand. She just isn't like that. Oh, Silas. Poor, poor Lucy.'

Tears shimmered in Julia's eyes. 'This is just so awful. Imagine loving someone who would do that to you. And Nick...how could he do such a thing?' She bit her bottom lip and then looked unhappily at Silas.

'It's going to be so dreadful for Lucy when she finds out what Nick's been doing.'

'Yes, but you can't interfere,' Silas warned her.

'Silas, she's one of my two closest friends,' Julia protested. 'Lucy, Carly and I have been like sisters. I can't just stand by and let Nick destroy her.'

'What I've told you is merely, at this stage, the informed opinion of my source. What do you think will happen if you do tell Lucy and she refuses to believe you? Blayne is her husband. She's besotted with him.'

'But we must be able to do something.'

'Maybe I could sound out her trustee discreetly.'

'Marcus, you mean? Lucy hates him.'

'Maybe, but he's still the best person to deal with the situation on her behalf. I've told my source to double-check and then come back to me. Until he does we can't really do anything. Was Blayne supposed to pay any bills for this party of Dorland's?' Silas asked.

Julia frowned. 'No, we worked together with Dorland, and he paid for everything himself. I'm going to be more a hostess for him than anything else. But why are you asking me that?'

'If Dorland had given Prêt a Party money then it's pretty likely it would have found its way into Blayne's pocket—and then we would have a repetition of what happened in Positano.'

'No, Dorland has definitely paid for everything himself,' Julia told him, adding with relief, 'Thank goodness.'

Julia was still thinking about Lucy several hours later, when she knocked on the door of Dorland's suite.

'Julia! What—no fabbie jewels?' Dorland exclaimed as he opened the door to her himself and immediately examined her left hand. 'Don't tell me the engagement is off?'

Julia laughed.

'Not yet,' she answered mischievously. She had no intention of giving Dorland any kind of hint that she and Silas were actually married, and she certainly wasn't going to let him guess why.

Dorland pouted, and then batted what Julia saw were fake turquoise eyelashes at her.

'I thought he was going to load you down with heirlooms.'

'The insurers wouldn't let him,' Julia answered, straight-faced.

'You must watch that, Julia. There is nothing worse than a mean billionaire,' Dorland warned her, ignoring her comment.

'Silas isn't mean.'

'Oooh, so it is a love thang, then, is it? I thought so! Sex is all very well, but take it from me, diamonds are better.'

'Speaking of which, did the Tiffany necklace turn up?' Julia asked him.

'No, and Tiffany are being absolutely *howwid* to me about it. You wouldn't credit it. Still, we won't talk about that now. Not when all I want to talk about is my fabby party. Everyone is coming...a certain celebrity European princess, plus an even more celebrity Hollywood couple—you'll know who I mean. They are all so famous I'm not allowed to so much as breathe their names,' he added coyly. 'Just the whole of the A list are going to be here—even a certain international footballer and his wife are coming, and guess who they are bringing with them?'

'Er...who?' Julia asked dutifully.

'Only Jon Belton!'

Julia looked suitably impressed at the mention of the ultra-famous pop singer.

'Oh, Jules, I am just *sooo* excited,' Dorland exclaimed excitedly. 'It is going to be the party of the year—and of course *A-List Life* will have an exclusive on it. Now, sweet, down to business. I've already spoken to the hotel people and arranged for a piano, but you know, I was thinking—wouldn't it be fun to have the balloons printed with a piano motif—black balloons with a white piano, perhaps encrusted with just the teeny-weeniest bit of diamanté? So retro and so Liberace. I can see it now!'

So, unfortunately, could Julia.

'Do you think that's a good idea?' she asked cautiously.

'Of course I do. Why? Don't you?'

'Well, it could be just a tad over the top, don't you think?'

'Julia, I am Dorland Chesterfield—*nothing* I do could *ever* be too over the top,' Dorland told her theatrically.

'How's it going?'

Julia shook her head as Silas reached for her hand and held it firmly in his own. He had been waiting for her when she finally left Dorland's suite, and now they were walking back to their villa through the hotel gardens.

'Dorland is wearing false eyelashes—turquoise false eyelashes. Apparently he's going to be wearing turquoise-coloured contact lenses for the party. And he's going to be sprayed with fake tan.'

'I'm beginning to fear the worst,' Silas murmured wryly.

'He's had a shirt specially made for him by Roberto Cavalli, and he's going to wear a white suit.'

She could feel Silas starting to shake with laughter.

'Silas, it isn't funny. He's bought a white poodle—and a diamond- and turquoise-studded collar.'

'For whom?'

'The poodle, of course. At least, I assume it's for the poodle. I haven't told you the worst yet, though.'

'Could it be any worse?'

'Yes. He keeps on talking about Liberace—Silas, stop laughing. *Silas!*' Julia protested breathlessly as he suddenly stopped walking and pulled her towards him.

'We're almost back at the villa,' she told him huskily, as his hands moulded her against his body.

'I can't wait that long.'

His skin smelled of warm night air and that sexy indefinable smell that was just him, and his lips were cool and slightly salty as they teased and cajoled hers.

Julia looped her arms around his neck and traced the shape of his mouth with the tip of her tongue, glorying in the now familiar star-burst of erotic delight fizzing eagerly inside her. It wouldn't always be like this between them, of course; one day this fierce, intoxicating passion would become a warm and familiar comforting glow rather than something that still filled her with half-shocked delight. One day. A long, long time from now, when they were old…

Growing old with Silas. The rest of their lives together. How very lucky she was—and how very, very happy. She held him tighter, kissing him passionately, making a small soft sound of pleasure deep in her throat as she felt him start to unfasten her cut-offs and then slide his hand inside the opening.

'You're so wet...'

'Mmm, I know... Uhh. Ohh. Mmm, Silas...' Her body was already moving rhythmically against his caressing fingers, her own hand closing round him whilst she shuddered in pleasurable anticipation. He fitted her so well. Filled her so well, making her feel each time that she almost might not be able to take the pleasure of the depth and intensity of his thrusts, and yet at the same time miraculously somehow making her feel that she wanted to stretch, to have more and more of him.

'Silas, I'm going to come,' she warned him.

'No. Not yet. I want to watch you when you do...'

He removed his fingers, slowly and gently, and then kissed her tenderly, keeping her close to his side as they walked the last few yards to their villa.

CHAPTER NINE

JULIA lay in bed next to Silas, dreamily watching the early-morning sunshine stroking golden warmth onto his bare skin. Silas had the most perfect male body she had ever seen, and just looking at it—at him—filled her with such a deep well of wonder and happiness. She had never imagined that she would know this level of joy and fulfilment, or feel that her future stretched out in front of her in a rose-coloured pathway sparkling with gold dust. She was just so happy—and all because of Silas.

'I thought you said you wanted to be up early today, with it being Dorland's big day.'

'Mmm, I did,' she agreed reluctantly.

She was going to be tied up for most of the day, and they had agreed that Silas would leave her to do what she had to do whilst he got on with some work of his own. But not yet. Definitely not yet. She snuggled closer to Silas, drawing sexy shapes on his bare shoulder with the tip of her tongue and then, nibbling his earlobe and whispering in his ear.

'You've got to guess what I'm drawing, and if you're wrong you have to pay a forfeit.'

'Which is?'

'Either massage my feet or shag me.'

'And if I get it right and win?'

'You get to massage my feet *and* shag me,' Julia told him generously, before adding dreamily, 'I'm keeping a count of how many orgasms I've had with you.'

'What for? Comparison or posterity?'

Julia giggled. 'Well, it isn't for comparison—no one could compare with you, Silas. Do you think I should count all those little mini multiple "o"s I had last night as one or individually?'

As Silas moved, the bedclothes slipped down past his waist, revealing the thick hard jut of his morning erection for her adoring and admiring approval.

'How close are you to double figures?' he asked lazily.

'Mmm…with the multiples I'm over it, and without I'm just over halfway to triple.

Oh…that is so nice…' She exhaled heavily as his tongue caressed the nipple of the bare breast closest to his mouth whilst his fingers worked sensually on the other.

Drawing her with him, Silas lay flat against the bed, so that she was arched over him on her hands and knees.

Watching her excitement as she responded to the sure guidance of his hands, Silas was sharply aware of how unique she was. He had had sex, and he had had good sex, but he had never had sex with a woman who responded to him with the openness and enjoyment, the complete naturalness and the sheer happiness manifested by Julia. She showed him in so many different ways that having sex with him gave her pleasure and delight and made her feel good, and as a consequence of that she made him feel good. In fact she made him feel one hell of a lot more than merely *good*.

Her breathless 'Oh, Silas, look!' had him pushing aside his thoughts to obediently look down his own body to where she was straddling him, and slowly and joyously taking him into her inch by inch.

'Mmm, doesn't that look good? It feels good too... You are just so big!' she cooed delightedly.

Foolish, flattering words. But the insane thing was that Julia quite plainly actually meant them.

She eased down on him a little more, using her muscles to gently squeeze and then stroke his erection in a movement that made him close his eyes and fight for self-control.

But Julia obviously had other ideas, and he could hear her laughing softly as she took him deeper and held him harder, and his control exploded in the red heat of his need to drive into her over and over again, his hands gripping her hips as she moaned and writhed above him.

Outwardly she might look businesslike and in control but inside she was just a delicious boneless mass of sexually satisfied woman. Very sexually satisfied woman, Julia congratulated herself, as she listened to a very Notting Hill type who obviously fancied himself describing to her the birthday party he had attended in Venice earlier in the year.

'And we were all taken to the party on these fantastic gondolas along the canals. Everyone was in costume. It was terribly Thirties and decadent. I've heard that an American TV network is filming Dorland's party for one of those fly-on-the-wall docudrama things. Is it true?'

'I really don't know, Charles. You'll have to ask Dorland,' Julia answered truthfully.

'And which famous people are going to be here?'

'I haven't seen the guest list,' Julia replied. Which wasn't true.

'Julia—darling!'

Charles was shouldered aside by a trio of frighteningly stiff-faced women whom Julia vaguely recognised from school—not fellow pupils but their mothers. One of them, or so it was whispered behind closed doors, had not— as she liked to claim—been in her youth a high-priced model, but rather a high-priced whore.

'So clever of you to bag Silas.' Cold sharp gazes swept her from head to toe.

These women were part of the new social order—fifty-something divorcees, prepared to fight dirty in order to look more like thirty. While their ex-husbands used their money to replace them with younger models, these women used their divorce settlements to try and turn back time. And the better-informed ones sometimes actually managed it, Julia knew, thinking of at least half a dozen high-profile society hostesses who genuinely looked as though they had been able to turn the figure five into a three.

Unfortunately for them, though, these three were not among that half-dozen.

'Yes, isn't it?' Julia agreed, flashing them a very happy smile.

'All that money, and a title—and best of all, he's wonderful in bed.'

Scarlet and green was never a good colour combination on aging faces, Julia decided smugly, and she left them with their red faces and jealous eyes to go and see how things were progressing with the decorating of the large marquee which had been put up for the occasion.

All the invitations had specified that Dorland's guests were to wear either their own most 'papped' (papparazzied) outfit, or a copy of one worn by someone else. And Julia had privately predicted that at least half the female guests under thirty-five (and that meant all the female guests, since none of them was likely to admit to being older) would be wearing a copy of the designer Julien Macdonald's itsy-bitsy sparkly dress, as worn by a certain top international star when she upstaged the bride at a celebrity wedding. With this in mind, Julia had suggested to Dorland that they keep the interior of the marquee quietly elegant and in colours that would act as a foil to the cele-brated dress.

Dorland had resisted her advice at first, hav-ing fallen in love with the idea of mimicking a certain branded and banded couple's wed-ding, with gold throne-like chairs studded with fake jewels instead of the simple, plain cream-covered dining chairs Julia had suggested, dec-orated with glittery grey and black and white ribbon tied into bows.

When Julia reached the tented anteroom of the main marquee, the construction people were just finishing setting up the champagne fountain Dorland had fallen in love with, and Dorland himself was busy giggling with a bevy of ultra-thin leggy blondes, who all seemed to be clutching small hairy dogs.

The combination of shrill yaps—from both pets and owners—was positively eardrum assaulting, Julia decided as she hurried out again—only to come to an abrupt halt as she saw Nick standing blocking her path.

'I hear you really ballsed up in Positano,' he told her unkindly.

Julia didn't like being bullied, and she lifted her chin and told him sharply, 'Someone certainly did.'

She thought for a minute that Nick was going to challenge her to explain what she meant, but instead he looked at her left hand and said mockingly, 'He's still not given you a ring, then?'

'Actually, he has,' Julia semi-fibbed. After all, Silas had told her that he wanted her to wear the Monckford Diamond.

'I must say you've surprised me, Jules,' Nick drawled nastily. 'I wouldn't have thought you've got what it takes to hook a man like Silas. Has he told you about Aimee DeTroite?'

'Whatever Aimee may have been to Silas, that is now in the past,' she told him lightly.

'You mean Silas has *told* you she's in the past. So far as she's concerned she is still very much in his present and his future—but of course he won't have told you that.'

What had she ever seen in Nick? He was a loathsome, vile, repellent toad, and she hated him for what he was doing to Lucy.

'No, he hasn't,' she agreed coolly. 'But he has told me about you.'

'What does that mean?' Nick demanded.

'You know what it means. It means that Silas has checked up on you and the business. How could you do this to Lucy, Nick?'

'What have you said to her?'

'Nothing—yet. But I—'

'Jules—there you are. Have you got a moment?'

'Of course, Dorland.' Julia smiled, walking away from Nick to go and see what Dorland wanted.

*   *   *

Had Nick just been trying to upset her when he had told her about Aimee? Or did the other woman genuinely have grounds for claiming that she was involved in an on-going relationship with Silas? An *affair* with Silas now, in fact, since Silas was married to her.

Julia could feel her heart thumping painfully. She felt sick and dizzy from the mixture of anxiety and confusion and adrenalin hurtling through her veins. She was determined to hang on to her belief that whatever had happened before her in Silas's private life was his alone to know about, if that was what he wished. Aimee was certainly not the type Julia would have thought would appeal to Silas. But Silas had dated her. And Silas had appeared in one of those stolen videos. She had not seen the video, but she had read the gossip when the story had first broken earlier in the year.

Nick was a troublemaker, she warned herself, and Silas was entitled to have a past. A past, yes. But right now she needed to know that not only was she his present and his future, but also that she was going to be his *only* present and future! And she needed to know it because she was wildly, passionately and totally in love with him.

Because he was the best shag she had ever had?

How shallow was that? Loving someone was about more than a ten-second orgasm, surely? About more than even double figures of them. Loving someone involved things like respect, and wanting to share the rest of your life with them, in sickness and in health. It meant that being with them added an extra dimension to your life. It meant that they were the light that filled your life, the extra special someone without whom your life felt empty and for whom your heart ached.

And that was exactly how she felt about Silas.

When she eventually got back to their villa, Silas was waiting for her.

'Sorry I've been so long. Dorland was waffling on for ever about Jon Belton. I think he might have a crush on him. Oh, and Silas, guess what? Nick's here.'

'Blayne? Why?'

'I don't know. Dorland interrupted us before I could ask him. I can't understand now why I didn't realise how loathsome he is when I first met him. I told him we know what's going on, and how much I hate him for what he's doing to Lucy.'

'I thought we'd agreed that nothing was going to be said about that until it could be proved?'

'Well, yes. I know you did say that. But he made me so very angry, and it just sort of slipped out.'

'What do you mean, he made you angry?'

'Oh, he said that he couldn't understand why you wanted me, and he asked me if I'd asked you about your relationship with Aimee DeTroite.' Julia looked at him, but Silas had turned away from her.

His body language positively bristled with 'keep off the past' signs that sent a shiver of female anxiety icing down her spine. As a woman she could think of only one reason why he was making it plain he didn't want to talk about Aimee, and that was because he still had feelings for her. No woman ever minded about talking about a burned-out love affair, especially not when doing so might help to underline her besotted adoration for her current love interest, Julia reasoned, so it must be the same for men.

Therefore, by one of those lightening and complicated equations so familiar to the female mind, she was very quickly able to work out that Aimee plus silence equalled unrequited love—which, when added to physical frustration plus male pride, added up to marriage to her. And that equation, when totalled with her own sum of total love for Silas, plus insecurity, plus jealousy, plus uncertainty, equated to the chemical effect of a lighted match being dropped straight into a keg of gunpowder.

The result was immediate and explosive.

'You just married me because you can't have her, didn't you? She rejected you, and so to make her jealous you pretended to be engaged to me! Well, I don't care how many sexy videos you made with her, she's—Silas!' Julia protested as he started to stride away from her.

'What the hell is this?' Silas demanded angrily as he turned to look at her. 'You're my wife, not a federal judge, and besides…'

'Besides what? You've only had sex with her?'

Silas couldn't believe his ears. Did Julia really think that he…? Aimee DeTroite was a head case—totally off the wall and dangerous with it.

'Look, Julia, just ease off on the histrionics, will you? I married you—'

'And you shagged Aimee—the whole world knows that, and most of it has seen the video,' Julia told him nastily.

The vicious slamming of the door as Silas brought their argument to an end shuddered through the whole villa.

Dorland's party would be starting in half an hour, and it was time for her to go over to the marquee—even though she hadn't made things up with Silas, Julia realised miserably.

All the time she had been getting ready she had been hoping he would walk into the bedroom. But he hadn't, and her own pride would not let her go in search of him. After all, she had done nothing wrong.

She looked at her watch. She couldn't delay any longer. Even so she still dawdled in the villa's entrance hall, and dropped her bag on the tiled floor to alert Silas to her presence just in case he did want to make amends, but her husband maintained an obstinate absence and silence.

She must not start howling now, Julia warned herself as she opened the villa door, and she blinked fiercely, firmly straightening her shoulders.

Silas removed his frowning concentration from the e-mail he had just received on his BlackBerry for long enough to watch as Julia hurried away from the villa. She was wearing a long black dress that clung sensually to her body. Round her hips she had wrapped what looked to Silas very much like the Hermès scarf his mother had given her for her birthday, and over that she had fastened a heavy belt set with turquoise stones. The whole effect was *very* Julia, Silas decided.

His frown disappeared and his mouth started to turn up at the corners. She would look stunning in the Maharajah's jewels, and she would probably devise some innovative way of wearing them that would shock the purists rigid. The sound of his own laughter startled him, and then made him frown slightly as he put down his BlackBerry.

There was no getting away from the fact that Julia had the most extraordinary effect on him. By rights he ought still to be angry with her, but instead he was laughing—and he was tempted to drop the BlackBerry and race after her. She was the most ridiculous, infuriating woman there could possibly be, aggravatingly sunny-natured and welded to those rose-tinted glasses through which she seemed to view humanity. She was illogical and stubborn and sometimes just plain crazy. And she made him feel…

Feel? He did not 'feel' things. He analysed and dissected them; he applied practical reasoning to them—just as he had applied practical reasoning to their marriage. But how could you apply practical reasoning to a

woman who wanted to know if a multiple orgasm counted as one or not; a woman who
referred to your penis as a 'gorgeous, sexy
hunny-bunny of a shag shaft,' cooing the
words in between stroking and kissing it; a
woman who asked you in all seriousness if you
thought that, if she whispered a few words to
them, 'all the sperm in your baby gravy' would
paddle like mad to make her pregnant.

Practical reasoning and Julia were poles
apart—at opposite ends of any scale—which
was why she needed him to keep an eye on
her. And that, of course, was the only reason
why he was going to get showered and
changed and go and join Dorland's ridiculous
ego fest of a party.

It was nearly midnight, the party had been going on for hours, and she still hadn't seen any
sign of Silas—even though she had spent what
felt like the whole night looking for him.

'Julia.' She stiffened as she saw Nick ap-
proaching with a group of louche-looking
young men—the sons of some of Dorland's
older guests, Julia recognized, most of whom
looked rather the worse for drink.

'I've brought a few of your admirers over to say hello to you.'

The boys—for they were little more, Julia decided—blushed and brayed and generally behaved as male teenagers do under the influence of drink and raging hormones.

'Are you enjoying the party?' Julia asked them in a kind voice, at the same time looking round discreetly to see if she could spot Silas anywhere.

'Any one for more champagne?' Nick demanded, revealing the unopened bottle he was carrying.

'Not for me, thanks,' Julia refused, showing him her already half-full glass.

'Rubbish—of course you want some,' Nick insisted, taking it from her and turning away to put it on a table while he opened the bottle, then filling it and topping up everyone else's glasses. 'Here you go.'

Julia took a polite mouthful of the drink and tried to keep up her smile as the men gathered around her, making drunken attempts at wit and charm.

'Has anyone ever told you that you've got great tits?' one of the boys asked her.

Pretending she hadn't heard him, she moved slightly away from him. She finished the champagne and put her glass down on a nearby table, wanting to get away.

'Is that Silas over there?' Nick asked Julia, and watched in satisfaction as she turned her head to look where he was indicating, towards the marquee.

In the darkness on the other side of the large people-packed stretch of gardens that separated him from Julia, Silas frowned as he saw her with Nick and a group of young men. As he watched, she put down her glass and seemed to be trying to edge away from the group.

She had her back to him, and something about her stance made Silas think of a young fox surrounded by out-of-control baying hounds. Blayne was obviously saying some-thing to her, because she suddenly turned her head to look in the opposite direction from the table. Behind her back, one of the group of young men refilled her glass while another dropped something into her drink.

Anxiously, and oblivious to what was happening, Julia continued to look in the direction Nick had indicated, even though she could see no sign of Silas.

'Julia!' Even though he knew she wouldn't be able to hear him, Silas still called out her name in sharp warning as he started to thrust his way through the crowd towards her.

'Come on, Jules—drink up,' Julia heard Nick urging her affably, as he proffered a second glass of champagne. Reluctantly she turned to face him, taking a polite sip. 'I really have to go now,' she told him. 'Dorland will be wondering where I am.'

'Oh, but we aren't going to let you go yet—are we, boys? Come on, drink up. That's right.'

There was a look in Nick's eyes that was quite frightening, Julia saw uncomfortably. A mixture of excitement and cruelty that made her desperately want to get away from him. And the boys with him, although no doubt charming as individuals, in their present overheated and drunken state reminded her far too much of hungry, mob-minded pack animals.

Nick was already holding on to her arm now, and the boys were pressing much closer to her than she liked.

Anxious to get away from them without any unpleasantness, Julia took a gulp of her champagne.

'Come on—you've got to drink it all. Hasn't she, lads?' She could hear Nick speaking, but oddly the words seemed to be reaching her from a distance. Even more oddly, her mouth seemed to be going numb, whilst her body felt heavy and all she could see were blurred images.

She was being sucked down into a vortex of darkness. Darkness and harsh mocking laughter, whilst hands reached for her and tugged at her clothes.

'What have you given her?'

Silas was standing cradling Julia's inert body in one arm, Nick's blood crimsoning the knuckles of his free hand, whilst Nick himself lay where he had fallen, in a tangle of wrought-iron chairs and pot plants, nursing his bruised jaw. The least drunk of the young men were rapidly sobering up, and looking white-faced with fear.

'Liquid X—you know, GHB,' one of them volunteered, shamefaced. 'Couple of doses, I reckon, 'cos Nick put some in too.'

Nick glowered at Silas silently.

'Blayne told us she was up for it,' another of them insisted. 'Said he'd see us all right if we helped him.'

Whilst Silas's attention was on them Nick managed to struggle to his feet. Damn that bloody bitch Julia. He had been determined to have his revenge on her, and to make sure that no one would ever take any accusations she might make seriously. If Silas hadn't intervened right now the Honourable Julia would have been on her way to becoming the Dishonoured Julia, in the cheap apartment Nick was renting. He had already set up everything he would need to film Julia enjoying the intimate attentions of the drunken youths he had planned to incite to take full advantage of her and the situation she was in.

By tomorrow morning he would have had a video of the whole thing that would have earned him a small fortune and humiliated and humbled Julia. No way would his sanctimonious wife have believed a word her precious friend had to say once his video became public property.

Silas could see Nick scuttling away, but he wasn't prepared to leave Julia to go after him.

He had reached her just as she collapsed, and had heard her terrified whimper of protest as she felt his hands on her body, her own trying desperately to push him away.

The images inside his head of what her fate would have been if he hadn't witnessed what was happening and got to her in time, filled him with fury and anguish. His arms tightened protectively around her as she lolled helplessly against him.

'You—go and find a doctor and bring him here,' he instructed the most sober of the youths grimly. 'There should be one at the first aid station. And as for the rest of you…I won't forget what nearly happened here tonight.'

CHAPTER TEN

SILAS stood sombrely beside the bed watching Julia as she slept. He had spent most of the night catnapping in an armchair so that he could both watch over her and be there should she wake and need him, and now the golden bars of morning sunshine striping the bed in honeyed warmth contrasted sharply with the darkness of his thoughts. Yes, Julia was here, and safe, but she might so easily not have been. And that would have been his fault. He could have made up their small quarrel before she had left the villa, but he had chosen not to do so, deeming it practical that she should be punished just a little for raising issues he did not want to discuss.

His fault. A surge of aching emotional anguish battered savagely against his once impervious belief in his own rightness.

Julia made a small sound and immediately he leaned towards her. The doctor who had seen her the previous night had assured him that there would not be any lasting long-term effects from the drug she had been given.

'But,' he had warned Silas gravely, 'in the short term it may well be that she will suffer from physical symptoms such as nausea and dizziness—and, more unpleasantly, emotional and mental panic, flashbacks, even paranoia. She will feel vulnerable and sometimes threatened. Fortunately, because you were able to rescue her, you will be able to reassure her that she has nothing to fear from what she can't remember.

'One of the most harrowing aspects of the way certain depraved and vicious men are using this drug against women is the fact that their victims cannot remember what happened. They have flashbacks, dream sequences of events, but these are shadowy and insubstantial, and it is my experience that a woman who has suffered rape via this kind of drug tortures herself over what she cannot remember as much as what she can. In fact, in one particularly traumatic and tragic case I had to deal with some months back, the young woman concerned actually took her own life. Your partner has been very fortunate.'

Silas made a small abrupt movement, unable to continue with his own train of thought, and then sat down on the side of the bed.

Immediately Julia opened her eyes and looked at him, starting to smile, her eyes alight with warmth and love. And then, as though a protective seal had been torn from her, her expression changed, all the joy leaching from it, as swiftly as dry fine sand running through a man's hand, leaving behind it an empty hollow that quickly became filled with darkness and pain.

Silas could see the fear and confusion filling her—sense it almost like a cold, thick, impenetrable fog. Automatically he touched her arm, wanting to comfort her, his heart thudding with the violence of his emotions as she recoiled from him.

'No, Silas, please,' she whispered. 'You mustn't touch me. Something horrible has happened.'

Her eyes were filling with tears and the look of agonised shame she gave him ripped at his heart.

'Julia, it's all right…'

'No. No, it isn't. You don't know what's happened.'

As she wept Julia lifted her hands to her face, pressing her fingers against her temples.

She felt so weak and confused, somehow aware that something unbearably dreadful had happened to her but unable to remember what it was. Images flashed through her head like lasers. Nick looking at her with a vicious cruel smile. Sounds: the braying laughter of men. Sensations. Hard male hands touching her. And, woven through them all, binding her with icy fear, the most terrifying and intense surges of panic.

'Jules, it is all right, I promise you.' Silas could hardly speak himself, his voice thick with a mingling of anger, guilt and an emotion he didn't recognise but that ran as pure as liquid gold, carrying only his desire to protect and comfort her.

'No!' Julia shook her head and wept. 'Nothing can ever be right again, Silas. You don't know what happened. Nick…'

As she shuddered and closed her eyes Silas took hold of her, binding her to him. 'Nothing happened,' he told her thickly.

'Yes, it did. But I can't remember what. All I can remember is that Nick made me drink some champagne. I didn't want to, but he insisted. And then...I can't remember what happened, but I know it was something horrible. And I'm afraid... You'll have to divorce me, Silas.'

'What?'

'I've heard about things like this happening...women being drugged and then... You don't know what's happened, because you can't remember, but you just get sort of flashbacks, and the men always claim that you were willing... Nick hates me, and if he...if they...'

The look in her eyes shocked and tormented him into speechlessness.

'If there were to be a child...' she whispered rawly, hanging her head. 'I don't know if I could—'

'Julia, you mustn't torment yourself like this. There's no need. Nothing happened!'

'You keep saying that, but you don't know—'

'I do know! I saw Blayne slip the drug into your drink. By the time I got to you it was too late to stop you from drinking it, and you were on the point of collapsing, but that was all that did happen.'

'But I will never know that, will I?' Julia told him quietly. 'I'll never know if that's true or if you're just saying it to protect me. And I'll have to live the rest of my life wondering if you're married to me because you want to be or because you feel honour-bound to be. I can't do that, Silas. I can't live like that. And I can't bear thinking about what might have happened. They *were* touching me!' Julia wept. 'I felt their hands…'

'Those were my hands.'

Julia pulled away from him and looked up at him, her eyes dark with despair.

'Julia, I give you my word that what I am telling you is the truth. I understand how you must feel, and why you feel it, but I have to say that I don't like thinking that you neither believe me nor trust me.'

'I feel afraid, Silas, and…and dirty. And… How can I ever have sex with you again when I don't know what might be happening inside my own body? When I don't know what might have happened—what things could—'

'Your body is no different this morning than it was yesterday afternoon when you left the villa. I am not in any way unwilling to have sex with you, Julia, because I know there is no reason for me not to do so other than my concern for you. And if you want me to prove that to you…'

'Where is Nick now?' Julia asked, without responding to his challenge.

'I have no idea. Dr. Salves has already advised me that if you want to press charges against Blayne, then—'

'No!' Julia stopped him violently. 'How can I do that when he is married to Lucy?' she demanded, adding weakly, 'My head hurts, and I feel sick…'

She was trembling almost violently, and Silas didn't waste time, simply scooping her up out of the bed and carrying her to the bathroom.

*   *   *

Julia looked out of the bedroom window towards the patio area of the villa, where Silas was sitting beside the pool, wearing only a pair of shorts despite the fact that it was already almost dusk. She could hear his voice, although not what he was saying, as he spoke into his BlackBerry. It was nearly a week since she had been drugged. Dr. Salves had told her two days ago that physically she was fully recovered, and she had told him truthfully that her feelings of acute panic and terror had begun to lessen. But, despite that, she was still haunted by the fear that Silas, out of kindness, had lied to her when he had told her that nothing had happened to her.

A little shakily she turned round and headed for the open patio doors.

When he saw her walking towards him Silas switched off his BlackBerry and stood up without moving, letting her walk to him instead.

'Silas, tell me again what happened with…when… I can't bear it that I can't remember!' She choked out in a tortured voice, stepping back as Silas reached out for her.

'Nothing happened.'

'You keep telling me that, but how can I believe it when I can't remember? How can I know that it's the truth and that you aren't just saying it to protect me?' Julia demanded emotionally. 'Dr. Salves says I may never have total recall, so how can I know if I can't remember?'

She flinched as Silas took hold of her left hand, clasping it between his own, but he refused to let her go.

'When I married you I took on certain responsibilities,' Silas began sombrely.

'Yes, I know, and it's because of that that I'm afraid you are just protecting me,' Julia burst out.

'One of those responsibilities,' Silas continued, as though she hadn't spoken, 'at least for me, is to ensure that our relationship, our *marriage*, has the strongest foundations it can possibly have. And for me the strongest foundations any relationship can have are those of trust and honesty. Trust is a two-way thing, Julia. A person may give it freely, or it may have to be earned. But both the person who gives it and the one who takes it have an irrevocable duty to honour it. I trust you to honour our marriage because I know the person you are, and I know without it having to be said that having married me, you will give your responsibilities to our marriage and to me priority above everything else. I give you that trust because I know that I can—because, if you like, I *know* you.

'And I promise you that you can have the same trust in me. Yes, I do believe it is my responsibility to protect you, and I blame myself for not being there to prevent what happened right at the start. But I would not be protecting you now if I lied to you about what happened and left your fears and doubts to fester. A clean, sharp, open wound always heals better than one that is hidden away. Had you been physically abused in any kind of way I would have told you. But you were not. I reached you as you collapsed and the only hands to touch you were mine. You were not abused, and you were not raped, and that is the truth. I promise you that on my word as your grandfather's heir. I cannot give you back the memory you have lost, but I can and do give you my promise that you can and will always be able to trust me to tell you the truth—just as I already know that I can and do trust you to be equally honest with me and for me.'

Julia's eyes stung with bittersweet emotional tears. How could she reject the precious gift Silas was offering her? She remembered how only this morning she had twisted away from him, refusing to let him kiss her, explaining reluctantly that she still felt contaminated and afraid, even though Dr. Salves had assured her that she was perfectly healthy.

'Julia?'

Unable to speak, she shook her head and then turned and ran back to the villa.

From their bedroom Julia watched as Silas walked to the far end of the pool. The subtle nightscape lighting illuminated the privacy of their enclosed patio and pool area and showed her the clean hard lines of his body, the strongly toned width of his shoulders that she had loved so much because they were so male and made her feel so safe, the nicely muscular firmness of his torso, arrowing downwards in a perfect V shape. Silas was muscular enough to look healthy and fit without looking mirth-provokingly like a contestant in a Mr. Muscle contest.

The shorts he was wearing, hip-hugging and long-legged, in black and white patterned cotton, were the kind favoured by surfers, and secretly she thought them far more sexy than the tight, skimpy posing pouches favoured by some men.

She wanted him so much, but at the same time she was filled with an unfamiliar sick fear at the thought of having sex with him. Silas might assure her that neither Nick nor anyone else had raped her, but Nick had certainly raped her of her delight in her physical relationship with Silas. And that physical bonding was such an important part of what had made things good between them.

But was she really going to let Nick do that to her? Was she really so weak and doubting that she was going to let him destroy their marriage? Or was she strong enough to trust in Silas, to truly trust in him from the depths of her being? The choice was hers.

Outside, Silas was swimming lengths with a powerful driving crawl that barely rippled the surface of the water.

Julia stepped back from the window.

Marriage obviously changed a man's thinking at some deep and profound level, Silas decided. There was certainly no other practical explanation for the way he was feeling and behaving right now. Logically, until Julia had overcome her present problems, it made sense for him to return to New York, where he had any amount of work waiting for him, rather than remain here. Practical explanations and solutions must always be any right-thinking man's preferred choice. And yet here he was, ploughing up and down a swimming pool, trying to work off the physical ache of his desire for her, and totally unable to find any kind of exercise that would do the same for the mental turmoil he was experiencing.

To say that he felt guilty and helpless and filled with savage anger came nowhere near to describing just what he did feel. He wanted to take Julia in his arms and hold her protectively safe. And at the same time he wanted to take her with his body and somehow bring back to life the happy, sexy, joy-filled lover who, he was only now beginning to realise, had completed and satisfied him as no other woman ever had. He wanted to tell her that nothing could ever happen to make him want to end their marriage. It couldn't; he simply couldn't envisage his life without her. But he also wanted to tell her that he ached and needed to have back the Julia she had been—the Julia who had laughed and joked and filled the hours they shared with her own special unique sunshine. And he missed that sunshine just as he missed waking up in the morning with her cuddled up against him, just as he missed that special feeling of male satisfaction and triumph that came with holding her tight whilst their heartbeats slowed to post-orgasm normality.

It seemed incredible to him that he could think of nothing and no one else other than Julia, that she filled his thoughts to such an extent that there simply wasn't room for anything or anyone else. It was because she represented a problem that needed a solution, he told himself. Because the way things were now was interrupting the smooth flow of the life and the future he had planned for them. Because this morning, when she had backed away when he had tried to kiss her, her eyes filling with tears, he had damn near wanted to cry himself.

And practical men did not cry. They found solutions instead.

'Silas...'

He stopped swimming in mid-stroke and rolled over to float and look up to where Julia was standing at the edge of the pool, wearing a sleekly fitting swimsuit that dipped to a deep V at the front.

'I thought I'd come and join you.' She held out her arms and told him, 'Catch me.'

The feel of her body in his arms as she slid into the water brought his aching tension into full-on hard urgency. She had pulled free of him and started to swim away from him, but she was nowhere near as powerful or skilled a swimmer as he was himself.

Taking a deep breath, Silas kicked down with a powerful enough stroke to carry him underwater towards her. His fingers closing round her ankles, he pulled her down to him.

The scent of the night air combined with the silky warmth of the water and the touch of Silas's hands on her body would once have been enough to have her virtually orgasming at the very thought of the pleasure in store for her, Julia thought bleakly as she closed her eyes, but she was helplessly aware of the empty nothingness that numbed her.

Wrapped tightly against Silas, she felt the powerful upward surge of their bodies as he kicked down and sent them up to the surface whilst her breath escaped in a stream of small bubbles.

Silas was kissing her, and mechanically she responded, her lips parting obediently, her eyes closing, her body as still as the soft air as his free hand gently caressed her and then closed over her breast.

Immediately she broke away from him, and swam towards the shallower end of the pool where she could stand up.

Silas followed her, taking her back in his arms. His body felt warm and heavy against her own, and a small shiver of something that wasn't either despair or pain flickered to life inside her. Hope or uncertainty? Did she really want to know which?

Determinedly she pressed closer to him, refusing to allow herself to draw back from the hard pulse of his erection. Instead she made herself draw a mental picture of his hardness, drawing it with the love and happiness she could remember but not feel. Warm, amorous mental brushstrokes of delight and excitement created a mental image of firmly muscled maleness, fleshed in skin that shaded from creamy olive to arousal-flushed deep rosy red, ridged and veined to bring it to three-dimensional power and life instead of flatness.

Inside her head she imagined herself touching it, stroking and kissing it, licking its shiny tight head. And all the time she was giving herself a mantra. This is Silas. This is Silas. This is Silas…

And this was Silas who was pulling her so close to him, slipping the straps of her swimsuit from her shoulders and baring her breasts and the protruding stiffness of her nipples to the soft glowing light, Silas bending his head to kiss her.

She flung her own arms round him and returned his kiss with passionate desperation. He broke the kiss, his hands cupping her breasts and his mouth caressing first one and then the other, bathing her cooling skin in delicious wet heat whilst Julia waited, checking and monitoring herself, tensing herself against the flash of memory she was dreading and the surge of fear and loathing it would bring with it.

Silas was guiding her out of the pool towards the comfortably cushioned loungers. Picking her up, he placed her gently on one of them, then reached for a towel and began to dry her with it, removing her swimsuit as he did so. Each touch of his hands was a caress that he made deliberately increasingly intimate, until her body was moving helplessly against his touch. He was taking her to a place she was afraid of going because of what she might find there, but she couldn't stop him because her own body didn't want her to stop him.

He had removed his own swimming shorts and her gaze fastened eagerly on his erection as it strained impatiently from the thickness of his body hair.

He knelt over her and she reached out to touch him, but he evaded her, parting her legs with his hand and bending his head over her. His lips brushed the sensitive flesh on the inside of her thighs and delight rippled through her. His tongue stroked upwards, and of her own accord she stretched wider to meet it, sighing happily in aroused anticipation as he folded back the fleshy outer lips of her sex and stroked the full length of her with his tongue-tip. Beneath its urgent stroke she could feel her clitoris swelling and pulsing. She cried out to him, joyfully giving herself over to sensation, the fear that had stolen away her sexual sense of self swept away by the sheer intensity of what she was feeling.

There were no hidden demons, no dark places, waiting to destroy her. There was only this, and Silas, and an overwhelming need to share with him her joy in the pleasure he was giving her.

*   *   *

'That was wonderful.' Her voice trembled and her eyes were wet with tears of completion and relief.

They were lying side by side on the sun lounger, and Silas leaned over her, gently kissing the tears from her face before brushing her mouth with his own.

It had been wonderful, he acknowledged, wonderful, wondrous, and perfect. He just wanted to lie like this, holding her and giving thanks for what she was and what she had given him, for the rest of his life.

Earlier, when he had entered her, complying with her achingly sweet urgent demands for him to thrust deeper and faster, he had been flooded with the most profound sense of awe and humbleness. And when, seconds later, he had spilled himself hotly into her, that feeling had become ever more intense and meaningful.

She was his soul mate, the only woman who could ever move him to such heights; without her his life would be meaningless and empty. Was this what people meant when they said they loved someone? Was this awesome, intense experience what love was? Was this...*love*. Was he *in love*?

CHAPTER ELEVEN

JULIA smiled contentedly as she slipped her feet into the funky shoes Silas had pointed out to her earlier in the week when they had been in Marbella.

Then she had laughed and refused to be tempted, but this morning she had weakened, and decided to slip into Marbella whilst Silas was catching up with some work—a necessity, he had claimed, now that they had been in Spain for over six weeks.

Technically there would have been time for them both to return to their respective homes and spend some time there before the beginning of November, when Julia had to leave for Dubai and the post-Ramadan party, but Silas had felt that it made sense for them to stay in Marbella, where neither of them was likely to be put in the uncomfortable position of having to lie to anyone about the fact that they were already married. Plus they would have the added advantage of being together.

How could she have argued with that when she loved being with Silas so very much? When, in fact, being together with him just went on getting better and better? Not even the pleasure of trying on such beautiful shoes could come anywhere near matching the dazzling, breathtaking happiness being married to Silas gave her. Just thinking about it filled her with a fizzing, bubbling joy that had to be the emotional equivalent of the world's very best champagne. She had never known anything like it. She woke up each morning with her heart dancing in eager delight, and she fell asleep in bed every night knowing that all she wanted in the world was contained in the man lying there with her.

Emotionally she felt as though she were living on a different plane, and every bit of her radiated with the happiness she felt. It awed her that after all the men she had met and dated who had not been right, Silas—who was—had been there in her life all the time. Wisely she acknowledged that what she had suffered because of Nick had actually helped her to see just how fortunate she was to have what she had found with Silas. She felt so incredibly blessed and fortunate. She knew that Silas felt Nick should be pursued and punished via the courts for what he had attempted to do to her, but she knew too that he understood and accepted that she would not do so for Lucy's sake.

Silas. She had already been away from him for far too long and she was missing him. She looked down at her feet. The shoes were lovely. And then out of the corner of her eye she saw a small display on the other side of the shop. Tiny, perfect replicas of the shoes she was trying on, made for little baby feet.

Her heart skipped a beat and then gave a rapid flurry of small, excited and eager thuds. Her eyes were misty with emotion. Silas's baby; their baby. If she felt deliriously happy now, how on earth was she going to feel when ultimately she conceived Silas's child?

She went up to the tiny shoes and touched them with a tender fingertip. How very sweet they were.

'You want?' the salesgirl asked, but Julia shook her head.

'Not yet,' she told her, as she handed her the shoes she did want to buy.

Not yet—but maybe soon? Silas would want an heir and her grandfather would be delighted if she were to make him a great-grandfather, especially now.

Julia smiled at her taxi driver when he pulled up outside the main entrance to the Alfonso, tipping him generously and considering whether or not to go into the club and order a cool drink or to hurry back to the villa to see Silas.

Did she even need to think about it? Of course not.

She didn't bother trying the front door of the villa, going instead to the small half-hidden gate that opened into the garden, just in case Silas had finished working and was sitting by the pool.

When she saw that he wasn't, she crossed the patio and opened the patio door, then stopped in shock as she heard a female voice she recognised saying, with cool sharpness, 'Silas, I can't believe that you've done this.'

'And I can't believe that you've flown all the way from New York to tell me that, Mother,' Julia heard Silas respond, equally coolly.

What was Silas's mother doing here? And what did she mean?

'Of course I haven't. Julia's mother wanted to talk to me face to face about the wedding plans, so I flew to London to meet her. She wanted to know if I thought she had missed anyone off the guest list and who else I might want to invite. She's trying to keep the list down to five hundred names because Amberley Church is so small.'

When Silas did not respond to her dryly given information she continued briskly, 'She also told me that you and Julia were here in Marbella—Julia, it seems, keeps in better contact with her mother than you do with yours. And, since I was already in England, I decided that I might as well fly home via Spain so that I could find out what exactly is going on.'

'You know what's going on,' Julia heard Silas retort dismissively. 'Julia and I are getting married.'

'Where is Julia?'

'In town. Buying shoes.'

Julia winced a little as she heard his mother sigh. She had always secretly suspected that Silas's mother thought of her as foolish and lightweight, and her sigh seemed to confirm that.

'Silas, I had hoped for better than this.'

Julia felt her heart take a high dive and plunge downwards with sickening speed. It was worse than she had feared. Silas's mother did not think she was good enough to marry him.

'There is no better wife for me than Julia,' Silas answered curtly, his defence of her making Julia's heart soar up again.

'I meant better *from* you, not better for you,' his mother responded immediately, causing Julia to go into semi-shock. 'And you know that. When you informed me on Julia's eighteenth birthday that you planned to marry her not because you loved her but because from a practical point of view she was the perfect wife for you, I told you what I thought.'

'You said that you didn't believe Julia would accept me,' Silas agreed.

His mother's visit had come as a total surprise, adding more complications to what was already a very delicately balanced situation. He and Julia were married, but as yet no one knew. Julia naturally wanted to tell her mother and grandfather before they went public, and equally naturally she wanted to do it in person. Silas had given consideration to flying back to England before they went to Dubai, but at the moment he was reluctant to share Julia with anyone else at all. Plus, he had wanted to see her restored to her pre-Blayne sunny happiness before plunging them both into the emotional storm the news that they had married in secret was bound to cause—especially with Julia's mother.

And then there had been that final consideration to make him hold back—that sharp, thorny, and very steep belief journey he had had to make from his denial that love was a concept even worth including in his calculations to admitting that it was a force that had rewritten his emotional and mental rule book.

Admitting to himself that he loved Julia had been the hardest thing he had ever had to do, and doing so had left him feeling acutely exposed and vulnerable. He needed more time to get accustomed to this new aspect to his personality, to feel comfortable with it and himself before he could go public and start telling the world that he was passionately in love with his wife. And he was damn certain that the first person he was going to tell was not going to be his mother. Especially not when those three small words he had been mentally sweating over for the last four weeks, whilst he imagined himself whispering them to Julia, had not actually been said yet.

Nope; so far as his mother was going to know, the status quo was exactly as he had told her it was going to be all those years ago.

But there was one thing he could safely say.

'Julia *is* the perfect wife for me.' Perfect in every way, but most of all in the joy she had brought into his life and the love he had for her.

Outside in the hallway, hidden from their view, Julia battled fiercely with her own feelings. Silas's mother's revelations had shocked and hurt her. But perhaps there was more of Silas's practicality in her than either of them had realised. Either that or his attitude had begun to change the way she thought herself, she decided bleakly. Because honesty compelled her to admit that Silas had never said that he loved her. She had simply assumed that he must because of her own feelings for him—and because it had never occurred to her that he would marry her for any other reason.

Now she could see that she had been hopelessly naïve. So what was she going to do now? Throw an emotional tantrum and blurt out that she loved him? Demand a divorce because he didn't love her?

But what was love? Did it always and only have to be the hearts and flowers outward trappings of romance familiar to everyone? Couldn't it sometimes be something else? Perhaps…something like a practical man protecting the woman who was his wife. Like that same man scrupulously ensuring that he secured her future and that of their children. Like that same man giving a high priority to their shared sexual pleasure. Were these things not in their own way a form of love? Or was she deluding herself? Trust and honesty were to be the foundations of their marriage, Silas had told her. She had accepted that she could trust him. Could she accept the sharp bite of his honesty as well?

'Well, right now, Silas, my concern is not how perfect a wife Julia will make you, but how happy a woman you will make her. I intend to wait for her to return, and when she does I intend to make sure that you have not pressured the poor girl in some way into agreeing to marry you…'

Julia took a deep breath, and then, before she could change her mind, she stepped out of the shadows and into the room, saying lightly, 'I'm afraid I've been eavesdropping. I got back a few minutes ago, and didn't want to break up your mother-and-son chat, but…' Was her smile everything he wanted it to be? Calm and serene and very much that of a woman who admired the man who wanted to marry her because it was practical to do so?

'I have to say, mother-in-law-to-be, that everything Silas has said makes perfectly good sense to me. In fact I totally share his feelings. I think we have more than enough in common to make our marriage work very well.'

'But you are not in love with him?'

'Being in love is not necessarily a prerequisite for a good marriage,' Julia answered Silas's mother firmly.

So far Silas hadn't said a single word, and when she looked at him she was surprised to see that he was looking back at her almost blankly, as though somehow what she had said was unwelcome to him.

Automatically she moved closer to him and reached for his hand, before saying huskily, 'Silas, I think we should tell your mother the truth.'

She *knew* that he loved her?

'The truth?'

'Yes,' Julia agreed, facing her mother-in-law determinedly as she said quietly, 'We haven't told anyone else yet, but actually Silas and I are already married.'

Julia watched as Silas's mother's gaze dropped suspiciously to her stomach and then lifted to Silas's face before switching back to her, and her own face grew pink as she read all the unspoken messages those three looks contained.

'No, he did not *have* to marry me,' Julia burst out indignantly, speaking the unspeakable as only she could, Silas decided ruefully.

His mother might have wrongly assumed that they had married in such haste because they had discovered that Julia was pregnant, but he doubted that she was likely to guess the real truth—which was, as Silas himself had only just come to recognise, that he had rushed Julia into marriage because quite simply he loved her and wanted to tie her to him in every single way that he could.

'You might have backed me up when I told your mother that you didn't marry me because I was pregnant, instead of laughing,' Julia complained crossly to Silas as he poured her a cup of tea.

It was just over an hour since they had returned from seeing Silas's mother off on her homeward flight, and Julia had begun to feel very tired.

'I was in shock,' Silas told her dryly.

'*You* were in shock?'

'I hadn't realised that you had such a practical turn of mind.'

Julia knew immediately what he meant.

'Well, I could hardly tell your mother that I wanted to marry you because you are quite simply the world's best shag, could I?' she asked lightly.

No way was she going to spoil what they had by bursting into tears and begging Silas to say that he loved her.

'Maybe not in those exact words,' Silas conceded. 'Although I dare say she would not have been averse to hearing that you feel passionately about me.' He knew that he certainly wouldn't.

'I do. Like I just said, I feel passionate about you being the most wonderfully orgasmic shag.'

Why did that make him ache inside with pain instead of with delight? Why was he suddenly feeling that sex on its own wasn't enough, and that he craved a connection with her that went deeper and was more profound?

'You don't think she'll say anything to Ma or Gramps, do you?'

'About shagging?'

'No. Silas, you know what I mean. Your mother won't tell them that we're married?'

'No. Although I must admit I don't really understand why you actually told *her*.'

'I thought from the way she was acting that she might actually drag me back to New York with her to save me from you,' Julia told him lightly.

'And you didn't want that?'

No! I want to spend the rest of my life with you and I can't bear the thought of living any other way, Julia thought. But of course she couldn't say that to him.

'Not really. Did you?'

'What? And miss being woken up every morning by you holding a one-to-one conversation with my penis? What do you think?'

'I think that the best place to drink a cup of tea is in bed.' Her world might have come crashing down around her, but, Julia reminded herself sturdily, no one else was going to know that.

'Mmm, nice thought—but maybe later,' Silas told her lightly, immediately standing up. 'I've got some e-mails to send...'

'To Aimee?' she challenged jealously.

Immediately Silas frowned. 'Why on earth should I want to e-mail her?'

When Julia made no response, Silas exhaled and told her grittily, 'I have no desire to either e-mail Aimee DeTroite or to bed her, if that's what you're worrying about. I do not want her, I have never wanted her, and I would not want her if she was the last woman left on earth. So far as I am concerned she is a neurotic whose behaviour borders on being dangerously de-structive—to herself and to others. Now, if you don't mind, I need a break from all this emo-tional self-indulgence.'

Julia put down her cup so that Silas wouldn't see how much her hands were trem-bling. He might have denied wanting Aimee, but he had also rejected her hint to him that they have sex as well.

As he walked away from her Silas told himself that, feeling the way he was right now, there was no way it made sense to take Julia to bed. If he did he couldn't guarantee that he wouldn't be able to stop himself from showing her that sex simply wasn't enough for him any longer. And no way did he want to do that after she had made it plain that it was all she wanted from him.

The irony of what had happened made him smile bitterly. He had been so wrapped up in his own desire to marry Julia for practical reasons that it had never occurred to him to question her motives for marrying him.

CHAPTER TWELVE

'I've sorted everything out with the travel agent. Apparently Sheikh Al Faisir is going to provide us with a private villa in the grounds of the Jumeirah Beach Club.'

Silas had been dealing with the arrangements for their trip to Dubai, and Julia nodded wanly as she listened to him, trying to concentrate on what he was saying. She had felt so nauseous this morning when she woke up, and yesterday as well, and now she just felt so incredibly tired.

'The Sheikh is connected to the ruling family of Dubai, and this post-Ramadan party we are doing for him will be attended by members of that family as well as his corporate guests,' she explained briefly.

'It's going to be a pretty grand affair, then?'

'Very much so,' she agreed, abandoning her mental attempts to backtrack over the last few weeks and work out some all-important dates. 'We suggested to the Sheikh that we keep to a glamorous Arabian Nights-based theme for the décor, with a sophisticated exotic fantasy element. For instance, the party is being held on a private beach with access to some of Dubai's most exclusive hotels. The guests will be able to sit and eat inside specially designed pavilions. They'll be covered in richly coloured silks and velvets—the whole effect will be rather theatrically over the top and very lush. Sort of Cecil B DeMille meets Bollywood, only much richer.

There'll be the usual fireworks, and those things that produce strawberry-flavoured smoke—they're really big over there. We've got a floorshow as well—magicians, sword-swallowers, a snake charmer, all that kind of stuff—and a belly dancer—the real thing. She's a superstar over there in her own right. They take belly dancing very seriously. It's a complete art form, of course. And we've got live music, and a guest list that includes loads of famous names from the horse racing scene and the pro golf world, plus quite a few Formula One stars. Then there are the celebs who have bought property out there on the

Palm Islands. Over a thousand guests have been invited in total. It's a hugely important contract for us.'

'And a very profitable one too, I should imagine.'

'I hope so, for Lucy's sake. She sort of hinted that it was Marcus who got us the business.'

'Blayne is not likely to turn up, I hope?'

'That wasn't the plan. We only got the contract after we'd drawn up the schedule for the year. Both Lucy and Nick were already involved with other projects, which is why I got it.'

'So where's Blayne now?'

'I don't know.' Julia started to frown. 'It's rather odd, really, because although I've spoken to Lucy pretty regularly she hasn't mentioned him at all.'

'According to my source, he isn't in London—or at least, if he is, he isn't living at home.'

Julia didn't want to talk about Nick. She had far more important and personal things on her mind. Was it nearly five weeks since she had last had a period or was it closer to six? And if it was closer to six did that just mean that she was late, or did it mean something else? Her heart bumped against her ribs.

'Silas, I... There's something...' she began huskily, but he was looking at his watch and exclaiming urgently.

'Hell—is that the time? I'm going to be late teeing off if I don't leave now.'

And then he was leaning over to give her a brief kiss before heading for the villa door.

Julia sighed ruefully. Was she pregnant? She certainly hoped so. Perhaps she should go into Marbella and buy a home pregnancy testing kit before she started getting too excited and making announcements to Silas. But first she had some work to do.

Silas had been gone just over an hour, when Julia heard someone knocking on the front door of the villa. Thinking it might be their maid, coming to see if they wanted the fridge restocked, she padded barefoot to the door and pulled it open.

An impossibly thin white-blonde young woman, with equally impossibly large unmoving breasts, was standing outside, a heavy fur coat draped over one arm and a tiny snakeskin handbag clutched in the diamond-encrusted fingers of her other hand.

Julia recognised her immediately.

'Aimee DeTroite.'

'I have to see Silas,' she burst out, pushing past Julia and marching into the villa. 'Where is he?'

'He—he isn't here,' Julia told her. It was the truth, after all.

'You aren't that aristocratic distant relative he's engaged to, are you? No, you can't be. Silas hates brunettes. He adores elegant blondes. Where is he anyway? I can't wait to see him and tell him our news.'

Their news—what on earth did she mean? Anxiety was beginning to tighten its grip on Julia's body.

'You *are* related, aren't you? He can't possibly marry you. He's going to have to marry me instead. You see…' Aimee paused for effect before announcing, 'I'm having his baby.'

Julia felt as though a trap door had opened under her feet, sending her hurtling downwards into sickening darkness. Don't you dare faint, she warned herself grimly.

Trust. Trust and truth were the foundations on which their marriage was going to be based—Silas had told her. And she had believed him because she knew that she could. Somehow she was going to find a way to hold on to that belief now.

'Really?' she heard herself saying. 'How very interesting. Are you sure it's Silas's?'

The puppy-brown eyes hardened into cold little pebbles.

'Of course I'm sure. Otherwise I wouldn't be here. I love Silas and he loves me, even if he refuses to admit it. He's all I've ever wanted. He knows that. We are destined to be together. Our souls have sped together through time and space to bring us here now. My astrologer has done our charts. He says he has never seen a couple so harmoniously linked to one another. I told him that our son will be a Lord...'

'An earl, actually,' Julia corrected her flatly.

Could it be true? Could Aimee be having Silas's child? Her belly was so flat and her body so thin that it didn't seem possible for her to have so much as a pinhead inside her, never mind a baby, but appearances could be deceptive. Her own stomach was still concave at the moment.

'If I were you I'd start packing right now,' Julia heard Aimee telling her smugly. 'After all, there's no point in making things harder for yourself, is there? I mean, Silas is not going to want you around, is he? He'll have to marry me now that I'm having his baby. Naturally a man in Silas's position needs a son, and I know that my baby is going to be a boy.'

It wasn't in Julia's nature to be manipulative or deceitful, but rather shockingly she heard herself announce calmly, 'Well, I'm afraid if you want to see Silas you'll have to go to London.'

'London? I was told he was here.'

'He was, but his mother stopped over a short time ago and asked him to go to London to attend to some business for her.'

'So when will he be back?'

'I don't know. He said not to expect him until the end of next week.'

'Next week? I've got a manicure booked the day after tomorrow. Whereabouts in London is he?'

'He normally stays at the Carlton Towers,' Julia told her truthfully.

'You won't be able to keep him, you know,' Aimee warned her. 'Silas is mine, and I'm going to have him—no matter what it takes. Where do I get a cab?'

'From the hotel.'

'You mean I've got to walk back there in these?' she demanded, displaying thin high-heeled lizard-skin shoes for Julia's inspection.

'Manolos?' Julia guessed appreciatively.

'Sure. I get the same design as the Hilton woman, only mine are higher. But then I guess my bank account is bigger than hers as well.'

Your ego certainly is, Julia reflected acidly. 'I'll walk back with you if you like.'

Anything to get rid of her before Silas got back.

'Sure. You can carry my coat for me. I had it specially made. There's this guy who breeds these special cats with long fur...'

Julia's stomach heaved.

Silas couldn't love this woman, she decided. It was totally impossible. Apart from anything else, there was something unwholesome and skin-pricklingly not quite normal about her.

Because she was anxious to get rid of her, Julia took a short cut to the hotel. It took them past one of the swimming pools which had been emptied prior to being cleaned. Julia was careful to avoid stepping too close to the tiled edge—more because of her companion's high heels than anything else—and her attention was on the weight of the heavy coat she had been forced to carry, so the sudden sensation of someone pushing her caught her off guard, causing her to cry out as she felt herself losing her balance. As she cried out she felt herself being pushed towards the empty pool, and the crazed violence in the brown eyes staring into her own as she turned her head towards Aimee in shocked disbelief turned her whole body cold with horror.

Aimee was trying to hurt her.

Neither of them had seen the three workmen who had come to finish cleaning the pool and now saw what they thought was one woman trying to help another as she fell. Of course they immediately rushed to help, grabbing Julia just as she was about to slip over the edge of the pool at its deepest end.

Julia didn't risk waiting for Silas to return to the villa. She was waiting for him when he came off the golf course.

'What is it? What's wrong?' he demanded as soon as he saw the anxiety in her eyes.

'Aimee DeTroite came to see you,' Julia told him.

'What?'

She could see how shocked he was.

'Do you love her, Silas?'

She had to know before she could tell him anything else. She had to hear him say the words—even though she felt she already knew his answer. Or at least she knew the answer the man she thought he was would give.

'What?' he repeated.

'I said, do you love her?'

'No, I don't,' he told her grimly.

I will always be honest with you, Silas had told her. She had believed him then and she believed him now. Very slowly she let her pent-up breath leak out of her lungs. Silas would not lie to her. Whatever she did not know, whatever she could not trust, she knew that and she trusted him.

'Aimee says she loves you, though, Silas. And she says—'

Silas cursed audibly—something Julia had never heard him do before.

'We can't talk properly about this here. Let's go back to the villa. She isn't there, is she?'

'No. I told her you had gone to London.'

'Thank heaven for that. Julia, I don't know what she's said to you, but I promise you she means nothing to me—'

'And I believe you. But she seems to think the two of you are fated to be together.'

'She's an obsessive. A while back, in New York, I began to feel like she was stalking me.'

'Well, according to her she's done a lot more than that,' Julia told him lightly as she unlocked the door to the villa.

'Like what?' Silas demanded.

Julia turned to look at him. 'She told me that I would have to give you up to her because she's having your child.'

Julia waited to hear him tell her that it was impossible. When he didn't, something inside her felt as though it was breaking in two.

She wasn't a child. She knew that men had sex with women for a wide variety of reasons that had nothing to do with having an emotional connection with them. But somehow she had thought that Silas was above all of that.

'She's crazy.'

'But it is possible that she *could* be having your baby?'

They were inside now, and Silas had closed the door.

'Yes,' he said carefully. 'It is possible.'

There were any number of dignified responses she could have made, but for some reason she chose instead to say, overbrightly, 'Oh, what fun! Because it just so happens that I think I might be pregnant as well. I wonder which of us will produce first? Her, I suppose.'

And then she burst into tears.

'Are you feeling any better now?'

Julia nodded her head. She was tucked up in bed, and Silas was sitting on the bed beside her.

'But explain it all to me again, please, Silas.'

He sighed. 'Very well. Aimee is an obsessive, and some time ago she decided that she was in love with me. She started turning up wherever I went; she called my friends, she invited herself to events she knew I was attending. She even tried to bribe my doorman to let her into my apartment, but thankfully he refused. She got into the boardroom at the Foundation and was found lying naked on the table—she claimed I'd told her to wait for me there. Luckily I was out of the country at the time. She sent me letters and photographs—'

'And videos,' Julia put in.

'Yes. It got to the stage where I was thinking about getting an injunction against her. I found out she had a history of mental problems, a compulsion/obsession complex that her family had kept hidden, so I told them that if they didn't get her some kind of medical help then I would.'

'Would you have done?'

'Probably not. But I didn't know what else to do to get rid of her. And then one evening when I was at a fundraiser she turned up. I was talking to one of my old frat buddies when she came over to join us. He started talking about when we were at Yale and how a few of us had been persuaded to donate sperm to this doctor guy who was setting up a sperm bank—supposedly to provide women who couldn't have children with sperm from intelligent, healthy men from good families. I can't believe now that I was ever credulous enough to believe that. I guess we were all going through some kind of idealistic phase. Anyway, Hal was saying how this doctor had expanded his donor bank and become something of a media personality, and that far from providing sperm free, as we had been told, he was charging thousands of dollars for it. Aimee joined in the conversation and started asking Hal questions about the doctor—who he was and where he was, that kind of thing. I suppose I should have guessed what was going through her head, but I didn't.'

'And now you think she could have bought your sperm from this doctor?'

'What I think is that she could have bought *someone's* sperm from him and convinced her-

self that it is mine—we were guaranteed anonymity, but, yes, there could be a small chance
that she may be carrying my child. Julia, don't
cry, please...'

'I can't help thinking about the poor baby.
Silas, we must do everything we can to make
sure it's going to be safe. Once she knows you
aren't going to leave me and marry her, she
might not want it any more.'

'Julia, it might not be my child.'

'But it might, and if it is it's only right that
we should do everything we can for it. Do you
think she'd let us adopt him, Silas? We could
bring them both up together? I can't bear to
think about the poor little thing growing up
thinking you don't care and feeling unwanted.
Even if she won't let us adopt him you can
make sure that he knows you, and that he
comes to stay with us...'

Silas started to shake his head.

'There'd have to be DNA tests first.'

'I don't think that would be a good idea,'
Julia protested.

'Why not?'

'Silas, Aimee is having this baby because she thinks it's yours. If it turns out that he isn't, she might just reject him. Then he'll have no one. You can't do that to him. It's too cruel.'

He had thought he knew her, Silas acknowledged, but now he realised that he had not known her at all. He had thought in his arrogance that he was her superior—intellectually, emotionally, and morally. Now he knew that the opposite was true. She had just shown him such a breadth of wisdom, such a depth of compassion and such a wealth of love that he felt humbled and shamed.

'You must think me the worst kind of fool for giving that damned sperm in the first place,' he told her bleakly.

Julia shook her head.

'No, I don't. Actually, Silas I admire you tremendously for it. It makes you human and caring. I think it is emotional and meaningful and a very special thing to have cared enough to want to give another person the gift of a child they cannot have for themselves.'

'Oh, Julia, don't. I love you too damn much as it is, without you making me love you even more.'

Julia stared at him, her lips parting.

'Would you mind saying that again?' she gulped.

A thin red tide was creeping up under his skin. 'Why?'

She started to pleat a piece of the bedspread with nervous fingers.

'Well, for one thing I want to make sure you actually did say that you love me before I tell you that I love you too. And...'

She was smiling at him, that lovely, light-filled Julia smile that felt like sunshine touching his heart.

'Did you really tell your mother you were going to marry me all those years ago?'

'Yes. But I didn't realise the real reason why I wanted to until a whole lot later.'

'How much later?'

'When all that mattered to me was seeing you smile again after Blayne had drugged you. When I knew that your happiness was more important to me than anything else in my life.

I knew then that it wasn't practicality, it was love.'

'But you told your mother…'

'I told my mother that you would make me the perfect wife. And so you do. Hell, Julia, I couldn't tell my mom that I loved you when I hadn't even told you yet.'

'You were so stiff and scratchy with me after your mother left that I thought you didn't want me any more.'

'I was scared stiff of touching you in case I lost control and told you how I felt. And how could I do that when you'd told me that you agreed with my reasons for marrying you?'

Julia reached up and touched his face tenderly.

'I love you so much.'

'Is there any chance of me having a practical demonstration of that?' Silas asked softly.

Julia gave an ecstatic sigh of happiness and held out her arms invitingly to him.

'No chance—just total certainty,' she managed to whisper in between the passionate kisses and hot words of love, with which he was claiming her as his own.

EPILOGUE

'OH, SILAS, look—it's snowing!'

Julia was snuggled up on the faded velvet-covered sofa, in Amberley's winter parlour, her six-month-old son, and eventual heir to Amberley and its history, lying fast asleep in his travel cradle next to her.

It had been Silas's idea that Henry Peregrine Gervaise Carter, to give him his proper name—or baby Harry, as his family called him—should be christened at Amberley Church on the anniversary of the day his parents had reaffirmed their marriage vows there. And of course Julia had been only too delighted to agree.

The birth of his great-grandson seemed to have given the Earl a new lease of life, and he was insistent that he intended to live long enough to sample the special wine he'd had laid down when Harry was born at his great-grandson's coming of age.

'It's early for snow. Oh, you don't really call this snow, do you?' Silas teased as he went to the window to look outside and then came back to sit down next to her. 'How's Lucy getting here? If she's coming by train, I could pick her up from the station.'

'I spoke to her earlier. She says she's going to drive down. I'm so glad she's agreed to be one of baby Harry's godmothers. She's had such a terrible time of it this last year. First finding out that Nick was having an affair and him demanding a divorce, and then all the problems she's had to face with the business.'

'Personally I think she's far better off without Blayne, although I agree that it can't have been easy for her dealing with the financial mess he left behind.'

'I wish she'd let you help her with that, Silas. I hate thinking of the struggle she must be having when we've got so much money.'

'She's got her pride, Julia, and we've got to respect that. I did have a word with Marcus, though, to tell him that he can always call on us to help her out. Where did that come from?' Silas demanded suddenly, as he saw the copy of *A-List Life* magazine lying on the floor next to Julia.

'I bought it when I went into town this morning,' Julia confessed. 'I haven't read it yet, though. I fell asleep after I'd finished feeding Harry. I have to tell you that your son has a very healthy appetite.' She reached down to pick up the magazine, flicked through it and then tensed, her eyes widening as she stared at one of the pages.

'Silas, look at this!'

'What?'

'This!' she told him, showing him the page that had caught her attention and reading aloud from it. '"One of New York's wealthiest heiresses announces her engagement. Millionairess Aimee DeTroite has just announced that she is to marry her personal astrologer, Ethain LazLo, the society stargazer who claims to be descended from Rasputin and who sports a similar hairstyle. Aimee and Ethain plan to marry on Twelfth Night, a date that Ethain has deemed to be predestined to unite them."'

'Well, I wish them luck with one another. They're certainly going to need it. Still, if he's as good at telling the future as he likes to claim, no doubt he'll already know what's in store for them.'

'Silas, that's not very kind,' Julia protested, but she didn't press the matter. She knew that Silas still felt angry about the way Aimee had behaved.

After claiming that she was having Silas's child she had refused to attend any of the medical appointments Silas's legal team had made for her, claiming publicly that she was afraid that the well-known and highly respected gynaecologist Silas had nominated to confirm her pregnancy was being paid by Silas to force a termination on her.

However, Silas's legal team had then spoken with the doctor who ran the sperm bank to which Silas had contributed his own sperm, and he had insisted that his donors' anonymity had never been compromised or their confidentiality breached, and that, whilst Aimee *had* contacted him and begged him to supply her with Silas's sperm, he had made it clear to her that this was not going to happen. In fact in the end, because he had been so concerned about Aimee's mental state, he had advised her that he felt she should undergo a course of extra counselling in addition to the pre-conception counselling all those to whom he supplied sperm had to undergo.

In a private letter to Silas he had further announced that in the fifteen-plus years since Silas had donated his sperm, technology had made such huge advances that he had decided to dispose of any sperm over three years old and start afresh. Therefore, even if he had been willing to help Aimee, he would have been unable to do so.

Four months after telling Julia that she was carrying Silas's child Aimee had announced via her lawyers that she had made a mistake and that she was not pregnant after all.

'You don't think that she was, and that once she knew that trying to force you to marry her wouldn't work she had her pregnancy terminated, do you?' Julia had asked Silas unhappily at the time.

'Trust you to think that—and to break your heart over it.' Silas had sighed. 'No, Julia, I don't think that—and neither do my lawyers.

I must admit I was surprised that Aimee didn't try to claim she had miscarried, rather than admitting she had lied, but the attorneys say that the reason she didn't do that was because her own lawyer would have advised her that if she did we could ask to see medical records as confirmation of her claim. Miscarrying at six or even seven months isn't like miscarrying at three, after all—we'd have been talking about the death of a fully formed child. Even her own lawyers admit that this isn't the first time she's tried to pull this particular trick. There was a similar situation when she was seventeen, but then she claimed the guy raped her as well.'

Baby Harry had woken up and was gurgling happily to himself. Immediately Silas reached down and lifted his son out of the cradle, holding him expertly in his arms. The look of doting male pride and love in his eyes made Julia smile as she watched father and son communicating with one another.

The anxiety they had suffered because of Aimee's lies had brought them even closer together, and to Julia's delight Silas had not only

been totally open with her, telling her everything that was happening, he had also asked
for her opinion and taken it on board, so that
all the decisions they had made had been made
jointly.

They were a team now, a unit, bonded
firmly together by their love for one another.

'I'll have the final arrangements to make for
the fundraiser when we get back to New
York,' she reminded him. 'I hope it's going to
be a success.'

New York's society hostesses had an enviable reputation for the excellence of their charity fundraising events, both in terms of money
raised and exclusivity, and Julia knew that
whilst on the surface she had been welcomed
and accepted by the wives of Silas's peers, the
success or lack of it at her first personally organised fundraiser was the real test she needed
to pass.

She had spent the last six weeks sitting for
the portraitist Silas had commissioned to paint
her wearing the Maharajah's jewels, with baby
Harry lying on her lap, holding one of the
priceless bracelets.

The portrait was to be unveiled for its first public viewing on the night of her fundraiser, along with the jewels themselves, and Julia felt that the jewels alone should guarantee her event was in a class of its own.

Her charity of choice was one for orphaned and homeless children, and she had deliberately chosen to have displayed, alongside her own portrait and some beautifully done photographs of the jewels, a set of hauntingly painful photographs of children living in the most desolate of circumstances—obscene riches portrayed alongside equally obscene poverty. Her aim was to raise for the charity a sum that equalled the ten million dollar value of the Maharajah's jewels—for surely no material possession should ever be held to be of more value than the life of a child?

'Thank you,' Silas murmured as he leaned forward to kiss her.

'What for?'

'For everything. I was right all those years ago. You *are* the perfect wife for me—perfect in every single way there is. And I love you more than I can ever find the words to say.'